"How b[...]
Spence moaned

Pulling Nan astride his hips, he turned wonder-filled eyes upon her perfection. "My lovely, elusive woman—in my bed at last."

"Not so elusive," Nan corrected gently. "No one knows me as you do." The palms of her hands slid firmly down his muscled chest. "Tell me again, Spence, that you love me."

"But you aren't listening," he said, his voice shaking with desire. "I love this mouth, these eyes...."

He pulled back the curtain of hair as she leaned to kiss him. "With every breath I'm telling you. With every touch."

THE AUTHOR

When she's not writing romance novels or short stories for *McCall's* and *Redbook*, Meg Dominique may be found bird-watching, gardening or hiking in her bright red sweat suit.

Meg loves to travel and has visited Europe, the Orient and every state in the Union except Alaska. Her trip to Prince Edward Island, Canada, was the inspiration for *Yes, with Love.*

Books by Meg Dominique

HARLEQUIN TEMPTATION
 2—WHEN STARS FALL DOWN
27—REBEL HEART
43—YES, WITH LOVE

These books may be available at your local bookseller.

Don't miss any of our special offers. Write to us at the following address for information on our newest releases.

Harlequin Reader Service
P.O. Box 52040, Phoenix, AZ 85072-2040
Canadian address: P.O. Box 2800, Postal Station A,
5170 Yonge St., Willowdale, Ont. M2N 6J3

Yes, with Love

MEG DOMINIQUE

Harlequin Books

TORONTO • NEW YORK • LONDON
AMSTERDAM • PARIS • SYDNEY • HAMBURG
STOCKHOLM • ATHENS • TOKYO • MILAN

For Joan and Anne
who told me about their island

———————————◆———————————

Published January 1985

ISBN 0-373-25143-2

Printed in Canada

1

AT FIVE MINUTES past three, Nan Blake rang the bell beside the tall front door and waited, trying again to imagine what Spencer Gallant would look like.

Remington Ware had told her only that a few of Gallant's excellent photographs had been on display in London recently and that the artist had the reputation for working only when he wanted to. It had even been necessary for her to discover that he made his home in this steeply gabled house near Malpeque Bay on Prince Edward Island—the end of the world as far as Nan was concerned.

But she hadn't minded tracking him down. The October foliage on her drive up from Boston through New Brunswick was the most beautiful she had seen in years, and if she could persuade the reclusive Mr. Gallant to provide a collection of his work for a January show at the Ware Gallery, Rem had promised her two weeks in Europe.

Nan wanted those two weeks. Davey was still

on temporary assignment in Paris covering top-level government talks between the Eastern and Western powers. According to the grapevine, he was dating Heather Bowen, an English model, but Nan was sure that if she could see him again they could patch things up and resurrect the marriage plans they had too hastily scrapped in April.

Beneath her feet Nan felt the porch floor quiver. Someone was answering her ring—a man, by his footsteps. She smoothed back the blond hair that brushed her shoulders. He would be sixty, she decided with a tremor of excitement. Heavyset and stern, **but** not intractable. She would charm the socks off **him** and be out of here by Christmas. Christmas **in Paris**—watch out, Heather Bowen!

Nan had her smile ready when **the door** opened. But except for the sternness that held his sensuous mouth in check, the man who looked back at her from across the threshold was light years away from being the person she was prepared to greet.

Angular and lean, he stood head and shoulders above her. If she was any judge of age, he was only a couple of years past thirty— and he wore a frilly apron!

Raising his wrist, he consulted his watch. "I'll give you two minutes." His deep-timbred voice cut crisply across the autumn air. "I have a cake in the oven."

Nan laughed. She couldn't help it. He reminded her of a Mount Rushmore carving decked out in ruffles.

His sternness deepened. "You have a minute and a half."

Hastily she apologized. "I'm sorry I've interrupted your baking." Apparently she had misread the amusement in his eyes, eyes so blue they put Malpeque Bay to shame. "I should have phoned before I stopped by."

"I'm sure you know that phoning is against the rules. I would have reported you for taking unfair advantage of your classmates. You could have said goodbye to winning that bicycle."

Suddenly his gaze narrowed as he focused for the first time on the outline of her trim body, flatteringly molded by a wine-colored wool dress neatly belted at the waist.

"I may report you, anyway," he muttered. "If you're fifteen, I'll eat my hat."

"I'm twenty-six." Nan brought her chin up, annoyed by his unabashed perusal. "And obviously I'm not who you think I am."

"I don't think you're anybody."

"*Every*body is *some*body!"

"Do you have a name?"

"Nan Blake." She eyed him squarely, wondering if the trip to Paris had just gone down the drain. "Are you Spencer Gallant?"

"It says so on the mailbox, doesn't it?"

"It says Spencer Gallant lives here. It doesn't say he has to be the person who opens the door."

"Particularly if he's wearing an apron? Is that what you mean?" His gaze lingered a moment longer on the high color that stained her cheeks. Then he stepped aside. "You'd better come in, Nan Blake. My cake is about to burn."

Nan's annoyance faded as soon as Spencer Gallant led her into his house. Its high ceilings and old-fashioned dark furniture could have been transported from her aunt's farm in Wisconsin, where she had spent the happiest summer of her childhood. A mirrored hat rack stood in the entry hall and in a corner of the living room she recognized a spinet of the same vintage as the one played by her aunt on evenings when they sang together. A bright hand-woven rug created a cozy sitting area in front of the hearth where a low fire flickered. A bouquet of winter fern and dried lilacs graced the mantel.

Nan paused in the doorway and breathed wistfully, "How lovely...."

Spencer Gallant watched her move into the room, his blue eyes following her graceful steps until she halted beside the sofa. "Sit down," he said. "I'll be back in a minute."

Nan watched him go, then perched on the edge of a needlepoint cushion, sniffing the air.

Chocolate and nuts. There actually was a cake in the oven!

But when Gallant returned he made no mention of it. He had taken off his apron, and as Nan gazed at the strong male lines of his body, enhanced by a pair of tweed trousers and a nubby gray sweater, she found it difficult to picture him again in that fancy piece of femininity that had startled her so when he opened the front door.

He settled in a chair across from her with the ease of an athlete and folded his arms across his wide chest. "Okay, Nan Blake from Boston, what can I do for you?"

In his absence she had practiced her introductory remarks, but the steady blue of his gaze drove them from her mind. "How do you know I'm from Boston?"

His lips twitched. "You have a foreign accent."

"Boston isn't that far away."

"Maybe not in miles."

Nan shifted uncomfortably, trying to figure out what his appeal was. He wasn't particularly handsome. His nose was too long, his brow too heavy. He had a chin like granite and probably a stubborn streak to match. Still, she felt drawn to him—to his eyes, to the mouth she had noticed right from the start, and to an indefinable quality of expression that worked like a magnet on her oddly alerted senses.

He was looking at her, too, concentrating his gaze first on the smooth sweep of her cheek, then on her small, straight nose and softly inviting lips.

Bringing her chin up, she met his appraisal head on. "As far as I've been able to tell, Prince Edward Island is—"

"P.E.I.," he broke in brusquely. "If you don't want to sound any more foreign than you already do."

"I was about to say that—*P.E.I.*," she enunciated stiffly. "Doesn't seem to me all that different from New England."

Amusement glittered in his stare. "How long have you been here?"

"Not long." She wasn't about to admit she had crossed the Northumberland Strait on a ferry only a few hours earlier. "But I've already done quite a bit of exploring."

"Is that so? What have you seen? McDonald's golden arches in Summerside?"

She wilted all at once. "All right, so I'm green as grass. But I'm not opposed to having the island's specialties pointed out to me."

He sat up. "Whoa. Hold it. Wait just a minute. Did somebody give you the impression I was a tour guide?"

"Hardly." It pleased her that she had shaken him up a bit. "In fact, no one wanted to tell me anything at all about you."

"Good." He relaxed again. "You can put that down as Number One on your specialty list. On P.E.I. we respect each other's privacy—at least after the tourist season ends." He eyed her pointedly. "And it has ended, you know."

"I'm not a tourist, Mr. Gallant." She tightened her grip on her briefcase and rose from the sofa. "I think what I'd better do is come back another time when you're more amenable to visitors."

His blue-eyed gaze held her where she was. "I think I'm probably as amenable now as I'm ever likely to be."

"I'm sorry to hear that."

The twinkle she had imagined before appeared again, leaving no doubt this time that it was authentic. "Have I been that rude?"

"Not rude, exactly." Reluctantly she obeyed the hand that waved her back down on the sofa. "But you do have a way of making a stranger feel not quite welcome."

"Only strangers who look at me as if I'm a crackpot. Am I the first gentleman cook you've ever seen?"

"Of course not. But you startled me when you opened the door."

"And you startled me. I expected a high-school girl peddling magazine subscriptions."

"Why?"

"Because that's the time of year it is. Leaves

change colors in October and high-school girls sell magazines."

"With a predictability you can count on when you answer the doorbell?"

"At this house you can count on it." He grumbled in the direction of a corner table piled high with glossy periodicals that looked unread. "Josey feels it's her personal responsibility to help every girl in the freshman class win a bicycle. Word gets around. They come in droves—when I'm shaving, when I'm putting on my underwear. . . ."

Josey. Nan experienced a twinge of unexpected dismay. It hadn't occurred to her that he might have a wife. But of course he did. A woman's touch was evident everywhere. He had been wearing her apron. She had arranged the lilacs on the mantel. Nan glanced at him again, wondering what there was about him that had made her think he was single. Not that it mattered. She was interested in his photographs, not his marital state.

"Mr. Gallant—" She broke into his muttered comments about the persistence of adolescent salespersons. "I've already taken a great deal of your time and I haven't explained yet what I'm doing here."

Unaccountably his look softened. "One thing you're doing is admiring my house. I have a feeling you've known a house like it somewhere else."

Her lips parted. "How did you guess?"

"I've been watching the way you keep stealing looks at the spinet."

For half a minute a hush enfolded them with an intimacy that warmed Nan like a hand on the nape of her neck.

"The house was my aunt's. In Wisconsin," she admitted. "My cousins and I used to sing old favorites after supper, and my aunt accompanied us on an instrument just like that one."

Strong-looking fingers steepled beneath the nose that now seemed to Nan exactly right for the masculine planes of his face. "You must have had fun in that house."

"I had a wonderful time." Nan's voice mellowed nostalgically. "They gave me a pet chicken I called Snow White—and I learned to milk a cow."

The smile that had been hovering on his lips widened into a devilish grin. "I suppose it's too much to hope that someone taught you to make seven-minute icing."

Nan stared blankly.

He stirred himself and looked at the clock on the mantel. "In exactly half an hour Josey's branch of the Ladies' Christian Service Guild is going to come trooping through the front door." A pained expression wiped away his grin. "I was supposed to have made that damned cake this morning. Do you think anyone will notice that it hasn't been frosted?"

Nan jumped to her feet. "I think everyone will notice! Why didn't you say you were expecting company?" Where was Josey? she wanted to know, but she said instead, "I'm no good at cooked frostings, but maybe I can help if you have some powdered sugar."

She hurried after him into the kitchen—a large, comfortable room that included a dining area and sitting room, as well. A pair of rockers rested in a bay window. Newspapers and books were strewn on the floor beside a sleeping white cat curled up in a yarn basket.

"One box of powdered sugar." Gallant pulled it triumphantly from a shelf above the counter where his slightly lopsided cake sat cooling beside a crusting Bundt pan.

Nan tied his discarded apron around her waist and began giving orders. "Wash that bowl and those mixing blades while I melt some margarine."

In a short time she was dribbling a creamy white icing over the peaks and valleys of Spencer Gallant's cake. He stood beside her, catching the overflow on the ends of his fingers and popping it into his mouth.

He told her admiringly, "This beats all to heck all that stirring and cooking."

"Yes, doesn't it?" Nan looked around dis-

tractedly and located her briefcase. "I have to
get out of here. The ladies are due any minute."

Gallant's eyes twinkled disturbingly. "Mariah
Pinkham is leading a lesson on the Book of Job,
I'm told. Visitors are always welcome."

Nan tried to ignore the unsettled feeling his
look inspired in her. "Another time, perhaps.
But I wonder if, before I leave, I could have just
one word with you about why I rang your doorbell."

"You can have two words if you like." A car
door slammed. "But not here."

Gallant took hold of her arm. "It's just occurred to me that it might be awkward explain-
ing to Josey how another woman got into her
kitchen before I even know myself. Come on."

He dragged her unceremoniously through the
back door and down a garden pathway where
heavy-headed dahlias nodded in a sea of color.
At the bottom of the garden he led her through a
gate and then closed it behind them. A pond lay
ahead. White ducks swam on it and a stand of
willows grew on the opposite bank.

When they got to the pond, Gallant pointed
out a bench and Nan sat down gratefully.
"There's never a dull moment with Spencer Gallant, is there?"

"I'm called 'Spence,'" he said, and let himself
down beside her, smiling. "You're winded.
What do you do, sit behind a desk all day?"

"Usually. When I'm not off in Canada pinning down elusive photographers."

"Oh. So that's it."

"That's what?" Working at his side in the kitchen, she had started to feel comfortable with him. She liked his unassuming naturalness. She liked the way he had made her feel about herself, as if there were something mysterious and femininely intriguing about her...something that might upset a man's wife.

She said with a coyness she didn't intend, "If you're wondering which of your P.E.I. friends squealed on you, none of them did. I was aware before I left Boston what your profession is."

He answered obliquely, "Then you're a step ahead of me. I don't know your profession."

"I'm an assistant to Remington Ware. At the Ware Gallery." Her heart began a faster beat. "Have you heard of it?"

"Modern paintings, West African art." His blue-eyed gaze cooled. "Yes, I've heard of it."

"We enjoy an international reputation."

"So I understand."

"We're known for representing only the best painters and photographers." Nan paused. "We'd like to represent you, starting with a one-man show of your work."

He asked in a disinterested voice, "When?"

"The end of January."

"No, thanks."

Nan stared. Nothing had prepared her for the calm way he had turned her down. "Just like that? 'No, thanks,' without even asking what our terms are? Without even considering what a show at the Ware Gallery could mean for your career?"

He turned his head slowly. "Just like that."

"I don't understand you!"

"Why should you? You don't know anything about me."

"I know you've exhibited in London. That makes you a professional. I think that courtesy at least demands a professional response to an offer from one of the outstanding galleries in North America."

The brief lecture amused him. "You take yourself pretty seriously, don't you?"

"I take my career obligations seriously." She thought fleetingly of the trip to Paris and saw it cartooned in her mind, on wings, flitting off into the breeze without her. "But obviously you don't."

"That's not entirely true."

"Then I think a snap judgment is not in order. I didn't expect a decision this afternoon."

"What did you expect?"

Plainly nothing would do with this man but straightforward answers. "I expected you to be flattered, first of all."

He eyed her evenly. "I am in a way. Maybe in a couple of years I'll be twice as flattered."

Nan wanted to tell him, *maybe in a couple of years you won't be asked!* But the situation was too precarious. She tried diplomacy. "You might be ready for a second showing by then."

"Not if I haven't had the first one."

Desperation prickled along her spine. She hadn't handled this well, not well at all. The only time she had been in command was the few minutes she'd been whipping up icing in Josey's kitchen!

"Before you say anything else," she told him, "let me fill you in on what Rem has in mind."

Spencer Gallant tipped his head. "Who is 'Rem'?"

Nan flushed at the thinly veiled criticism. "Remington Ware."

"Your boss."

"Yes." She took a breath to counteract his disapproving tone. "We're also, close friends, so we're on a first-name basis."

"I see."

The condescension in his reply angered her. "We're friends because he recognizes my capabilities, and I feel fortunate to be associated with him in a business that I enjoy and do well at. We are *not* good friends in the gossip-column sense of the word."

Gallant flipped a pebble into the pond. "Which means you don't sleep together?"

She wasn't prepared for his bluntness. "Mr. Ware sleeps with his wife!"

He turned a merry smile on her. "Something only a good friend would know."

Nan got to her feet. "I don't like the direction this conversation is taking."

"Neither do I. It's boring the hell out of me." Gallant stood, too, stretching in a leisurely way that made her feel stiff and foolish beside him. "Let's go for a walk."

"No, thank you. I'm going back to Summerside. I have some calls to make before dinner."

"Business calls?" He reached for her hand. "I'm disappointed. I thought I was your only assignment on P.E.I."

Nan hated the weakness in her body in response to his touch. "The Ware Gallery has two shows scheduled between now and the end of January. Both of them require my attention."

"It must be gratifying to be so important."

"Is everyone you meet subject to the blunt end of your tongue?"

"Only beautiful young ladies." Laughter showed on his mouth and in the crinkling skin at the corners of his eyes. "And only after I've already figured out that they can stand up to it."

"Maybe you're wrong about me."

"I could probably find out during a nice long walk. You could use the exercise, and you can't leave, anyway." He waved his hand back toward the house, and she saw with dismay that her car was blocked in by half a dozen others parked behind her in the driveway.

He took her arm again. "I don't imagine Mariah is any further along than Job's second case of boils. And they still have our cake to eat. Come on, be a sport. I'll show you something special down on the beach."

2

SPENCER GALLANT'S HOUSE stood on a slope above an inlet opening out into Malpeque Bay. A few miles back of it was the town of Bideford, a pleasant community of carefully tended homes. Ahead in the water to the left lay a small body of land called Lennox Island, with Green Point Provincial Park on the right across a narrow strait.

As they walked out over the browning fields toward the water, Nan's annoyance cooled. Gallant had said no to her offer, but her professional intuition—now that she had calmed down enough to let it function—told her it wasn't a definite no. There was still a good chance she might persuade him, and it was encouraging to think this walk might give her that opportunity.

He had overstepped the boundaries of good taste by inquiring into her relationship with Remington Ware, but he seemed to be a man who ignored formalities. He was too unconcerned about anything happening beyond the perimeters of his island to have any more than a mild curiosity about her personal life. He seemed to her a genuinely contented man, and she took a long look at him, thinking as she did that in her experience he was a rare specimen.

One of the problems that had led to her breakup with David Pryor was the restless ambition that drove him. In five years' time the man she had been engaged to six months previously had made himself a leading photojournalist with connections in Boston and New York. His work was known around the world. His reputation was secure, but he was too on edge about keeping it secure to take much pleasure in it, or in anything else that might infringe the slightest bit on his commitment to it.

Competition in his field was too keen, he had told Nan, for him to assure her positively that he would be on hand for the June wedding they had planned. They could be married in Paris, he had offered as an alternative. But when she had tried to pin him down on a date, he hadn't been certain about that, either. It all hinged on the talks. If they bogged down, he intended to ask for reassignment to the Middle East. If he went there, he had no idea when they could squeeze in a wedding.

Nan couldn't imagine "squeezing in" a wedding at any time. One either had time to get married or one didn't. Until Davey could put the same priority on their future as she did, there would be no wedding, she told him.

She returned his ring and canceled the caterer and the string quartet she had hired to play for the reception. She was lucky, she told herself. She had found out before it was too late that David Pryor was the wrong man for her. But she couldn't shake off the fear that she had made a mistake, and whenever she recalled the sunny April afternoon when she had said goodbye to him, she was impressed anew with how great her loss was.

Except for the unemotional way he had relegated his relationship with her to second place in his life, Davey was her ideal. Sophisticated, masterfully organized, witty. She would have felt unshakable as his wife. The domestic uncertainties that had hounded her parents' marriage and spoiled her childhood would never have hounded Mrs. David Pryor or upset in any way the beautiful flaxen-haired children she had hoped to have.

When Remington Ware offered her two weeks in Europe if she could convince Spencer Gallant to join the stable of artists at the Ware Gallery, all her old dreams came to life, clawing their way out from beneath the layers of rationalizations that had been her only means of survival during the critical weeks after Davey had left.

The trip would give her a chance to confront

Davey again in a less emotional state, a chance to find out more about Heather Bowen and to let Davey know she was willing to make allowances now for his insatiable ambition. He could never be as calmly unperturbed as the tall, lean man striding along beside her with the ocean in his eyes. But Spencer Gallant, she mused, was too far on the other end of the scale. Even if she was able to convince him to do a January show, she wasn't entirely sure that anyone with so little interest in furthering his career could ever live up to the promise that Rem believed Gallant's London exhibit held.

Spence spoke out as they neared the water's edge. "Lennox Island." He pointed out a curving bit of land glimmering in the sunlight. "It's the site of the Micmac Indian Reservation. There's a museum there and a church and a craft shop."

He looked down at her small, determined figure tramping along at his side. "As far as I know there aren't any Micmacs in the States."

Nan bowed to the note of irony in his voice. "Another vast difference between here and home," she conceded. "I'll give the Micmacs the Number Two spot on my list of P.E.I. specialties. Is Lennox Island what you brought me to see?"

He grinned. "Only from a distance. The immediate attraction is down there."

As they came out on the brow of the beach, Nan saw that the sandy stretch in front of them was alive with activity. Horse-drawn carts and pickup trucks were parked haphazardly over an expanse of several hundred yards, and hordes of men, women and children were busily at work filling them with a brownish-green substance they were collecting from the beach.

Nan stopped in her tracks. "What's going on? Has there been an oil spill?"

"Those aren't cleanup crews," Spence said. "They're enterprising fishermen and their families collecting P.E.I. specialty Number Three—Irish moss."

"Does it grow on the beach?"

"It grows in the ocean. A gale we had several days ago blew it ashore."

Nan watched the bustling activity below her. "The way they're going after it, it must be valuable."

"It's a harvest from the sea that they haven't had to work for until now. A free gift that will bring a nice profit when it's dried and carrageenan is extracted from it."

" 'Carrageenan'? I've never heard of it."

"There might have been some in the chocolate in Josey's cake. It's an emulsifier. It also has thickening and stabilizing properties that are useful in a variety of products such as shampoos and ceramic glazes."

Nan gazed at him, amused. "You told me you weren't a tour guide."

He gave her an abashed smile. "Am I boring you? This is an aspect of life here that's rather unique. I thought you might not want to miss it."

"You're right." Her tone softened. "Could we go down for a closer look?"

Gallant took her elbow to help her through an area of deep sand, but Nan noticed when the beach smoothed out that he kept his hold on her, and she wondered a little uneasily what the fishermen he hailed might think. Some of them were sure to be friends of Josey, too. But Spencer Gallant went around introducing her with no apparent self-consciousness, although her elbow was tucked securely against his side.

One of the women stopped work long enough to ask, "Is this your first visit to P.E.I.?"

Nan nodded. "And the first time I've heard of Irish moss."

"Then have some." Reaching into the bed of her truck she brought out a net bag and filled it to the brim before passing it across to Spence. "Have Josey make your friend a pudding," she said with a smile.

"Thanks very much," Nan said, but after the woman walked away, she turned doubtfully to Spence. Sand clung to the wet, furry mass that dripped from his hand, and its unappetizing color gave her a bilious feeling. "I can't imagine eating that!"

He laughed, showing a row of even white teeth. The wind ruffled his dark hair, and the blue of the sea had deepened the color of his eyes. "You'd be surprised how good it is when it's cooked and strained. It's like a blancmange, and it's loaded with vitamins and minerals."

"I guess it's not very sporting of me, but I think I prefer chocolate cake."

"Then let's go and see if the ravenous Ladies' Guild has left us a sliver."

"I was joking."

"I wasn't."

He led her firmly back across the sand, whistling a tune she couldn't quite place and enclosing her hand in his as if she were a child he had taken out for an airing and was dutifully returning home. However, he took a long way around, delaying them for a while in a copse of wild cherries in order to admire the bronzed leaves dancing in the wind.

"Tell me about the house in Wisconsin," he said.

Nan leaned against a tree and let herself be transported back to the childhood summer she had spent on her aunt's farm.

"It was heavenly," she replied. "Full of high-ceilinged rooms like your house and quaint old furniture with the knicks and scars of the ages

on it. I had a room under the eaves. I loved it
when it rained. Everything felt so permanent
there, so secure."

Spencer Gallant studied the wistful expression
on her face. "It sounds as if away from the farm
your life was pretty uncertain."

Normally Nan would have resented that kind
of personal intrusion. She had never discussed
the stresses of her early years with anyone. But
this intriguing stranger's concern struck her as
genuine and she heard herself going on with
only a mild reluctance.

"'Uncertain' is too weak a word. It was
chaos. My parents spent a number of years
working up to a divorce. The months before I
went to the farm they quarreled constantly. Of
course, some of the quarrels were my fault—a
lot of them were." She said to his quizzical look,
"I couldn't stand to see dad and mom angry at
each other. It seemed less painful somehow to
make them angry at me."

Gallant was quiet, considering what she had
said. "So they decided the farm was the best
place for you?"

She smiled thinly. "I felt terribly put-upon at
first. But it turned out to be a lucky thing. The
farm was wonderful, as I've said. It was the happiest summer I've ever spent."

Spence gave her a curious look. "You never
went back?"

"I couldn't. The farm was sold soon after I left." She picked up a red leaf and held it up to the sun. "It seemed to me when I was there that everything was perfect, but later I learned that my aunt had had almost as many problems as my mother. She certainly didn't need an extra mouth to feed."

Spence said lightly, "How much does a ten-year-old girl eat, anyway?"

The remark broke Nan's mood and she laughed. "This is getting maudlin, isn't it? The sad, sad story of Nan Blake's life. You might not have opened your front door today if you'd known what you were getting into."

He regarded her silently for an instant. "One of life's charms that I most appreciate is the unexpected." Then he took her by the elbow, commenting, as they started off again, on the unusual beauty of the autumn.

When they were once more in sight of the house Nan said, "I feel guilty that I've taken up your afternoon. I hope Josey won't mind."

"She took up most of it herself," he answered carelessly. "I spent an hour just trying to decipher the recipe she left me. Scalded milk," he scoffed. "Whoever heard of it? And then I had to hunt up all the bowls and the whisk and the measuring spoons."

"It's none of my business, but I can't help wondering. Why didn't Josey make her own cake?"

Gallant explained. "She has a part-time job at an antique shop in O'Leary. The shop's closed for the winter, but they had a break-in last night and she was called to help with an emergency inventory this morning."

"Oh, I see. She's lucky that you could fill in for her."

"Maybe." He flashed a smile that filled her with a dizzy kind of happiness. "We'll see how many of the church ladies are lying prostrate on the lawn."

Nan laughed. "I don't see a one from here. And all the cars are gone."

"Good. Peace reigns once more at the Question Mark."

"The what? The 'Question Mark'?"

"That's what we call the house." He stopped on the path and tossed a stick at the white cat, awake now and sneaking up on the ducks drowsing on the pond bank. "Josey and I can never decide which of us it belongs to."

Nan halted beside him. "What do you mean? The cat?"

He laughed. "The house."

"I'm thoroughly confused."

"It's not very complicated. Our parents died without leaving a will. I say the house is Josey's and she says it's mine. We've been fighting about it for nearly three years."

Nan stared. "Josey is your sister?"

"Certainly she's my sister." He gave her a quizzical look. "Who else would she be?"

"Your wife, I thought."

"My 'wife'!" He hooted.

"Is that so preposterous?"

"I guess it isn't to someone who doesn't know me. But anyone who does could tell you a wife wouldn't put up with me for five minutes."

The sinking sun slanted gold fingers across his hair and deepened the creases around his eyes.

Nan inquired carefully, "What's so terrible about you?"

"I leave my socks in the parlor. I scatter newspapers all over the floor."

Nan countered. "You also make cakes in emergencies."

"Only this once. Never before. Never again."

"You could be trained to pick up your socks."

"Ah—" He touched a light finger to the tip of her nose. "But I don't want to be trained. I've successfully resisted all attempts for years. I enjoy being slovenly. I like unmade beds and dirty dishes and crumbs on the table. If I smoked, I'd drop ashes on the carpets, too."

"There are women who wouldn't mind."

His expression stilled. "Are you one of them?"

"No." Her heart beat a strange tattoo. "I'm compulsively tidy."

"I thought so." He stood looking down at her, caressing her with his eyes. "Every hair is as much in place now as it was hours ago when you rang my bell."

Her hands went self-consciously to the blond swirl on her shoulders. "I'm sure that's not so."

"It may be an illusion," he agreed. "But it's a lovely illusion. Would you let me photograph you sometime?"

Nan was caught by surprise. "Why would you want to?"

"Because I like the way the light falls on the planes of your face. I'd like to catch whatever shy thing that is that lurks behind those bold brown eyes."

"I've never been called 'shy' before!"

"I'm not calling you 'shy' now." He curved his palm beneath her chin and lifted it. "I'm saying something shy hides inside you. Maybe I could lure it out."

Her heart hammered. "And what would you do then?"

"That remains to be seen, doesn't it?" He took his hand away, trailing it lightly down across the base of her throat. "May I photograph you?"

"Maybe. I don't know. I might head back to Boston tomorrow."

His low laughter mocked her. "Baiting the trap?"

She flushed. "Why should I say yes to you when you said no to me?"

"That's a good question." His blue eyes glittered. "Let's discuss it over dinner."

Nan hesitated, not entirely recovered from her impression that he was married.

"Where are you staying in Summerside?" he asked.

"I haven't booked a room yet. I thought if there was a possibility that we might be working together I'd try to find something closer to your farm."

His eyes twinkled. "Nobody told you that Josey and I rent summer cottages on the bay front?"

"Why should they have? It isn't summer."

"I can tell by your tone that you're thinking they're flimsy little four-sided matchboxes."

"I'm not thinking anything!"

"Nothing at all? A blank mind?" He made a clucking noise with his tongue. "I don't believe it. I can hear the wheels turning."

She tossed her head. "And what do they tell you?"

"They say if I'm offering you one of my cottages I must be planning to work with you."

The brown eyes he had called 'bold' snapped back at him. "Well, are you?"

He took her arm. "We'll talk about it at dinner."

3

WHEN SPENCER GALLANT and Nan came back into the farmhouse kitchen, his sister, Josey, was there, buzzing around in a flurry of dish-drying.

Nan's first impression was that she was a younger sister. She stood only a little taller than Nan and was trim and dark haired, with a wide smile and laughing eyes of the same clear blue as Spence's.

But when she came forward to greet Nan something in the way she moved and spoke marked her as older. Nearly forty, Nan decided, putting out her hand, wondering at the same time how it happened that someone so attractive was still sharing a home with her brother.

"Well, just look at the two of you," Spence said when they had acknowledged his introduction. "Except for your hair and a few years' difference in age, you could be two peas in a pod. You could wear each other's clothes."

Josey laughed. "You ought to have yourself fitted for glasses." But she said to Nan, "If you'll give me that beautiful dress, I'll trade you three of what I have on."

"You've made a bargain." Nan was comfortable at once with Josey's easy familiarity. "If I'm not mistaken that's an Irish fisherman's sweater you're wearing."

Josey nodded, pleased that Nan had recognized the worth of her dearest treasure. "I made a trip once to the Aran Islands."

"With our grandfather," Spence said. He took an apple from a bowl on the table and bit into it with a sharp cracking sound that brought a frown to his sister's face. "Josey had three offers of marriage and one to serve as a midwife before Grampa Turner could tear her away and whisk her home still in her maiden state."

Josey gave him a severe look. "Would you care for an apple, Nan?"

Spence grinned and held out the bowl. "I would have asked her myself, but she prefers chocolate cake."

"Oh, dear," said Josey. "There isn't a crumb left."

"Is that so?" Spence preened. "It must have been delicious."

Josey patted his cheek affectionately. "The cake was a bit lumpy, but the icing made up for it. Everyone wanted to know my secret ingredient. I had to tell them it was too secret to reveal. I hadn't the faintest idea what you'd done to it. It certainly wasn't what I expected."

Spencer grumbled good-naturedly, "What you expected would have taken all afternoon. As it was, we had fifteen minutes. Nan whipped it up."

Josey's expression showed a mixture of dismay and amusement. "Someone should have warned you about Spencer."

Nan smiled. "What would they have told me if they had?"

Spencer answered for her. "They'd have said, 'Never ring the bell at the Question Mark on baking days.'" He took hold of Nan's arm, a gesture she was beginning to hope wasn't as automatic as it seemed. "Come along, lady," he said, "it's time for your dinner."

"You're going out?" Josey's brow lifted. "Couldn't I fix dinner here for you?"

"Make up the spare room, instead," Spence said over his shoulder. "Nan hasn't decided on a place to stay, so she might as well bunk with us."

Nan pulled back. "I couldn't do that—"

"Why in the world not?" Josey dimpled. "I owe you one. If you'll tell me what was in that icing, I'll owe you two."

"A drop of peppermint and a teaspoon of almond extract." Nan hesitated. "Are you sure I won't be putting you out?"

"I'd consider it a blessing if you'd stay."

Josey's smile took on a wistful cast. "You don't know how I crave a woman to sit with by the fire."

Spence said dryly, "Don't wait up."

"It happens," Josey answered saucily, "that I have a date of my own. If you get home before I do, little brother, put out the cat."

"I LIKE YOUR SISTER," Nan said on the drive to Summerside. "She made me feel at home right away."

"Not like her brother, eh?"

Nan glanced across at the rocky outline of his profile. Despite her softening attitude about the length of his nose, it was still too long. But she warmed to the craggy look of him, to the confidence in his movements and the quick laughter that sprang up in his eyes. "You're not too bad when one gets used to you."

"Gee—thanks a lot. Maybe I'll buy you a lobster instead of a hamburger."

"Why don't I buy dinner for you and put it on my expense account?"

Spence gave her a sharp look. "That would mean you're entertaining a client."

"Rem makes allowances for prospective clients. You're entitled to eat lobster, courtesy of the Ware Gallery, without signing your name in blood."

"Then maybe I will."

"It's all settled, then."

"Dinner. Nothing else."

"Dinner is all we're talking about, isn't it?"

Darkness had fallen as soon as the sun had set. The wind outside had an icy edge to it and Nan felt warm and secure riding along beside Spencer Gallant in his bright-red compact car. It was nice, too, thinking about spending the night in his lovely old house.

Her thoughts drifted to Spence's suggestion that he photograph her and on to the remark he had made about something shy lurking inside her. It was a remnant of those lonely years after her parents' divorce, she guessed. She had felt it there herself, holding her back now and then when she preferred dashing forward, making her tongue-tied when she needed to be articulate. But no one else had ever commented on it, not even Davey, as close as they'd been for so many months.

Spence said, "Josey liked you, too."

Nan jumped at his voice cutting through the twilight. "I'm glad. Josey is a person one wants to please, isn't she?"

"I've never thought of her in exactly that light." He swung the car in a wide arc, up over a narrow bridge and down again. "There was a time, in fact, when I took a great deal of pleasure in driving her crazy."

Nan smiled. "How old were you then? Nine or ten?"

"Something like that. She had the same boyfriend then as she has now."

"Spence, that's incredible!"

"Umm. She should have married him years ago, but she didn't, and he married someone else."

Heather Bowen, faceless but bewitching, flashed across Nan's brain. "Obviously he isn't still married."

"He and his wife divorced a few years ago. It wasn't a good match to begin with. I think Beau felt sorry for her. Sorry for himself, too, probably."

"Because Josey rejected him?"

Spence nodded.

Nan knew she was asking too many questions, but she couldn't seem to stop. "What was wrong?"

"Our mother was ill." He let out a sigh. "She had a crippling case of arthritis and later, breathing problems. My father could have hired a housekeeper but he didn't. Josey felt it wasn't fair to keep Beau dangling indefinitely, so she broke off with him."

"Your mother didn't recover?"

"No, but she didn't die, either, not for a good many years. Josey settled in."

Nan couldn't help asking, "What did you do?"

"I grew up. I went off to Harvard."

"You have a degree from Harvard?"

He grinned across at her. "I have scars, but no degree. I got out just in time."

"What do you mean?"

"They were about to make a businessman out of me, with a tie around my neck and stock certificates up to my armpits."

"Isn't that what you went for?"

"I went because my father sent me. Two years later it dawned on me that I didn't have to stay, and I took off like a cannonball."

"Where did you go?"

"Everywhere my thumb could take me. I'd hitchhiked to Mexico when my father had a stroke. I came home to see what I could do to help, and I've been here ever since."

Nan was quiet the rest of the way into Summerside, aware of a peculiar resentment building up inside her, resentment mingled with sympathy for Josey, for Spence—sympathy for the way life sometimes was, but resentment for the way some people lay down and let it roll over them. Of course, in Josey's case, there were extenuating circumstances. A sense of duty, loyalty to a sick mother. But what could she say for Spence? He seemed to let the wind blow him where it would.

She was almost angry when he drove into the parking lot of the Brothers Two restaurant. But when he got out and came around to open the door for her, she was impressed once again with the easy, relaxed air he projected. People spent whole lives striving for the kind of calm contentment he seemed to have achieved without striving at all.

She gave him a puzzled smile as she stepped out of the car. "I don't know quite what to make of you."

He surprised her by answering seriously, "I don't know what to think of you, either."

"What's so perplexing about me?"

"That you're here," he answered vaguely, "about to eat lobster with me."

The wind whipped icily up her coat sleeves. "Is it that unusual for you to be taking a woman to dinner?"

He regarded her silently for a moment. "You're taking me, remember?"

NAN SPENT a comfortable night at the Question Mark. The room Josey had prepared for her was in a gable overlooking the bay and Lennox Island. There was a little tiled fireplace and beside it a bentwood rocker and apples in a wooden bowl on a reading table. The sheets were scented with dried lavender, and while the wind howled outside Nan snuggled beneath a down comforter and tried to ignore the questions she couldn't answer about Spencer Gallant.

But in the morning, sitting at the breakfast table with Josey and him and later, tramping with them across the frost-tipped fields, she felt as unsettled as she had when she and Spence had arrived at the restaurant in Summerside.

Dinner there had been a pleasant meal. The lobster was superb, and they had talked pleasantly for an hour afterward over wine accompanied by music. But they hadn't talked about her offer, as Spence had promised they would.

Instead, most of the talk had centered around

Spence's varied interests. Nan had encouraged him because she was fascinated. He painted, she learned, and made wood carvings of birds. He was also researching an Acadian history of Prince County, the county in which he still lived and in which ancestors on his mother's side had settled during the mass expulsion of Acadians from Nova Scotia in 1755. And of course, he was a photographer, but he talked less about that than anything else. When Nan veered back to it, he changed the subject, inquiring again about the summer she had spent in Wisconsin.

"When it was over," he said, "who did you go back to, your mother or your father?"

"My mother." Nan toyed with her dessert fork and decided not to tell him that her father had married again as soon as the divorce decree was final. "We had a difficult time for a while. She hadn't held a job since I was born, and it was hard for her to find an entry into the business world. When she finally did get a job, it wasn't much of one. Long hours and not much pay." A shiver rippled up Nan's spine. "I still remember how I hated the awful street we lived on and coming back after school to an empty apartment."

"What did you do to make the time pass until your mother came home? Watch TV?"

Nan shook her head. "I thought I was too sophisticated for the cartoons, and the talk shows were unsettling. The topics were above me, of course, but mainly I objected to all those people crowding our living room when they weren't really there."

Spence said softly, "Especially when you couldn't talk back to them?"

Nan glanced up in surprise. "That's twice today you've been amazingly perceptive."

"'Amazingly?'" He shrugged. "I don't think so. I'm often affected the same way by the wonderful boob tube. One-sided conversations have never appealed to me." His gaze touched her parted lips. "When you were with your mother, were you chief-cook-and-bottle-washer?"

She laughed. "Not cook. But my strong suit, as you can guess, was tidying up. I drove my mother crazy, lining up her shoes in the closet the minute she took them off and rolling all her belts into little round coils that had to be just so in the third drawer of her bureau."

She dropped her gaze. "I guess I was trying to make up for the messy details of my life that I couldn't do anything about, but it was a habit that stuck. I'm still an organizer and a list maker. I still have to plan out my days and know exactly where I'm headed."

Spence smiled lazily. "That's where you lose me. I don't want any part of anything structured. Imagine what would have happened today if I'd followed Josey's plan and baked her cake when I was supposed to."

Nan felt oddly reluctant to hear what she knew he was going to say.

"I wouldn't have been at home when you rang the bell." He slid his hand under hers and closed his strong fingers around it. "We wouldn't be sitting here. We might never have met at all."

"We would have." Nan took her hand away on the pretext of lifting her hair from under her collar. "You're at the top of my list for P.E.I. I would have hunted you down sooner or later. By the way—" she smiled brightly at him "—when do I get to see some of your work?"

"No rush." His easy smile moved from her eyes to her lips. "More coffee?"

It was the next afternoon before he finally took her upstairs to his studio in the attic, a large open loft that accommodated all his pursuits. A darkroom adjoined it, where Spence made his own prints.

When Nan stepped into the loft the first thing that impressed her was how neat it was. Clean, uncluttered, not a bit the hideout of the slovenly bachelor he claimed to be. But it wasn't the kind of neatness Josey practiced downstairs. The house Josey kept was all of a period, like a comfortable museum, its chief relics marking the milestones of the Gallant family.

But in Spence's attic the order was timeless.

Things ancient and modern, decorative and utilitarian, existed in arrangements that complemented their beauty. Beside a striking piece of Mexican statuary sat a couple of wooden lobster pots, as arresting in their useful simplicity as the lush Toltec nude their clean lines flattered. Paintings lavish with color covered one wall. The wood carvings were arranged on a table in much the same way they would have been in a marsh the birds foraged. There was one little plover Nan longed to cuddle in her hand.

Everything Spence created or collected had a magic to it, but what caught her eye and held it while everything else dimmed was a photograph of a church, hanging alone on a long wall facing the door. The lines of the small wooden building were starkly simple, but the shadows cast by the sunset behind it were so exquisitely composed, the balance between light and dark so perfectly controlled and yet so natural, that a shiver of excitement gripped her.

"Oh—" She could hardly breathe.

She knew now why Remington Ware had come home from London with nothing on his mind except making sure that Spencer Gallant was brought into his fold.

In the Northeast there were dozens of excellent photographers, most of them vying for Ware's attention. But none whose work Nan had seen was as creative as this artist. None had his eye for detail or the skill to capture it as he had done.

Superficially the photograph was of a church, but from the moment Nan saw it, she was plunged into a desire to know everything about the building's history from the day the first nail was hammered into it. The smell of its lumber involved her. The texture of the earth in the churchyard assailed her and a gamut of other reactions clamored forth as she continued staring at the photograph.

Noting how rapt she was, Gallant said, "That's one of a series I'm doing on the churches of the island."

All Nan could think of to say was, "Are there a great many churches?"

"Over two hundred." He went to the window and raised a shade. "But not all of them are interesting. The ones with the most character are the rural churches like this one."

Dimly Nan recalled half a dozen such structures that she had passed on her journey through the countryside in search of Spencer Gallant's house.

"I love the ornate trim," she managed to say. "It contrasts so strikingly with the simplicity of the basic lines."

Spence came back to stand behind her. "I'm fascinated by the contrast. I get lost in it. Josey

comes looking for me sometimes and finds me
stretched out in a church graveyard so deep in a
trance she thinks I'm as dead as everyone else
there."

The remark called for a laugh, but Nan was
too absorbed to respond appropriately. A feeling had come over her that she had lived her
whole life so that at this moment she would be
standing here, captured like a mote in sunlight
between Spencer Gallant and his work.

She turned around, half-dazed, and stared up
at him. His eyes traveled over her upturned
face. Then, as easily and confidently as he did
everything else, he put his arms around her and
kissed her.

Every thought left her mind. Her whole being
concentrated on his touch and his mouth moving on hers. Spencer Gallant held her as if he
were claiming what had been his always. When
he let her go after a minute, she stood away
from him, stunned to see that it was still a clear,
golden afternoon. Nothing had changed except
inside of her, where a vast, untethered yearning
bedeviled her blood.

"Lovely Nan." He touched her cheek. "Nan
Blake," he murmured. "Out of nowhere into my
life. . . ."

The haunting words acted as powerfully on
her senses as the touch of his mouth. They
seemed to tell her that he, too, had lived his

whole life for this moment. Desire uncoiled inside her. It took all the control she had to say, "I'd like to see more of your work, please."

Amusement flickered briefly in his eyes. "Which work did you have in mind?"

She pulled in her breath. "Your photographs, of course."

He moved languidly away then, toward a desk under the windows. She watched him rummaging around inside its drawers, still conscious of his hands sliding around her body, touching her with a possessive certainty that not even Davey in their most intimate moments had conveyed.

Startled, she heard him say her name again. "This is all I have to show you."

She went quickly toward the desk, where he had spread out eight or ten prints, a few of them of churches in the same vein as the one that hung on the wall. Others were of curling leaves afloat on a stream, of sea gulls silhouetted against the sky or caught in a mass effect as they gleaned a field. One shot was of Josey at a loom, her shadow predominant. One was of a pair of flattened shoes, toed in toward each other and speaking volumes in their misshapenness. Not sentimentally, but with a powerful objectivity that took its strength from the pure-white background on which they were photographed and the careful detail Spence had included.

All of the prints were marvelous. Beyond praise, Nan thought, searching for some way to tell Spence that she knew how special they were without sounding gushy.

But Spence seemed unconcerned by her silence. After a minute he swept the prints back into the drawer and closed it. "There's the answer to your offer," he said calmly. "A dozen photographs wouldn't make a show at the Ware Gallery."

"But surely you have more!" Nan stared at him. "Your work is so polished, so perfect. You've been working for years to achieve such quality."

"Working," he agreed, "and throwing away what didn't measure up."

"Not your negatives!" Nan was aghast at the possibility. "You haven't thrown away those!"

"Except for the ones matching what you just saw, I've burned every one of them."

"Why?"

"Why not? I know what I'm after. I'm not interested in anything less than what I'm aiming for."

"Even the lesser efforts of an artist are important," she protested. "Like the trim on the churches, they have a contrast value, they provide a record."

"My work stands or falls as it is when I declare it satisfactory. I'm not making compromises with my history."

His stubborn stance appalled her, but at the same time admiration was growing inside her. No one she knew in the art world was so bold. Davey's files were bulging with negatives that dated back to his high-school days. The writers she knew clung to even the most insignificant scraps of paper, anticipating the day when phrases culled from one piece of work might fit another.

She asked, "You've never regretted throwing anything away?"

He shook his head.

"You're that certain that you're the best judge of your work?"

"I'm the only judge who matters to me."

They were arrogant words, but there was nothing arrogant in his voice or in the way he moved from her side to stand studying the church print on the wall.

"One day I'll have a collection fit for showing in the Ware Gallery. But I don't have it now."

He could have, she knew. Out of the ton of work he must have burned, her practiced eye could have chosen fifty pieces at least that would have made up a splendid show. Not a show as perfect as Spencer Gallant had fixed as his goal. But artists sometimes worked a lifetime for that.

She could have wept for all that had been wasted, but still her admiration for him exceeded the regret she felt. It mingled inside her with the feelings his kiss had aroused and made her light-headed and unsteady as she went to stand beside him.

"What about the prints that are in London?"

"Those are sold."

"We could arrange to borrow them. Remember, too, that you have nearly three months before the show. Your collection will grow."

He put his hands in his pockets and turned around. "You don't give up easily, do you?"

"Since I've seen your work, I don't intend to give up at all. We'll figure out something. All that's keeping us from it is your reluctance to commit yourself."

"There isn't a chance in the world I could have a show ready by the end of January."

"What if—" Nan took an unsteady breath. "What if you had someone to help you? Someone to catalog negatives and assist with the cameras and do the darkroom work?"

"I like to do the darkroom work myself."

"I don't mean the printing. I mean the messy stuff, stocking it, cleaning up, the sort of thing that would free you for more important tasks." She didn't add that her talent to organize might help, too.

He observed her quietly. "Who did you have in mind?"

She breathed out slowly. "Me."

She was taking a long step out in the dark, she knew. She had never worked on a day-to-day basis with an artist before. She had no idea what the problems might be—or if such an arrangement was even feasible. There was Davey in Paris with Heather Bowen...there were other shows that needed her attention. But her lips still burned from Spence's kiss. The ache inside her hadn't gone away....

She met his gaze, hoping her uncertainty didn't show. "When I left Boston it was with the understanding that I might be gone until Christmas. I expected that there'd be mountains of work here to sift through, decisions that couldn't be made in a hurry. It usually takes a month at least to work up a proper catalog."

While she talked, his gaze intensified. He went to the desk and sat down on the edge of it. When her voice died away, he said, "I've never worked with anyone before. I don't know if I'd want to."

The objective response she ordinarily would have given wasn't there when she reached for it. He was the first client she had ever kissed, and now she was paying the price for behaving unprofessionally.

She hated the tremor in her voice when she spoke, as much to bolster herself as him. "The decision is up to you, of course. But I can't think you'd know until you try it."

"What if I try it and I still don't like it?"

She congratulated herself on the shrug she managed. "I won't keep plaguing you. We'll appraise the situation and I'll go home if it isn't working out."

She waited while he looked at her, hardly daring to breathe. So much depended on what he decided...the January show...her trip to Paris. And whether or not he ever kissed her again.

He said with a roughness foreign to her concept of him. "I won't consider it unless you agree to one condition."

Her staunchness unraveled into a tangled weakness in the pit of her stomach. He had sought to establish right from the start whether she slept with Remington Ware. She hadn't figured him for a man who might be sexually exploitive, but she knew nothing about the core of certainty within him, how deep-seated it was... or how demanding....

"What is your condition?"

"If I do the show, I'll do the church series for it or I won't do anything at all."

Relief mingled with a pinprick of disappointment that his prerequisite had nothing to do with her.

He laughed when he saw he had surprised her. "What were you expecting? That I'd demand hummingbird hearts for lunch every day?"

Nan put cold fingertips to her hot cheeks. "I think your idea is marvelous. It just over-whelmed me, that's all."

"I'll agree it's an overwhelming proposition. Narrowing the field down to one subject runs the odds way up that even if I agree to do the show, I won't be able to finish on time."

A surge of adrenaline made her bold. "Is that why you chose it?"

"I chose it because it's the only phase of pho-tography I'm interested in at the moment. It might be a good idea for you to give that some serious thought. Imagine the critics' reaction when they open the gallery door and see nothing but churches. You and your Rem could be tak-ing a terrible gamble."

Her experience in dealing with artistic tem-peraments reasserted itself. She could recognize a case of nerves when she saw one, even if it was buried beneath layers of quiet assurance.

"Does that worry you? What the critics will say?"

"No, it doesn't worry me. I've already told you, I'm the only judge who matters to me."

"That's easy to say when you're out here on your island with no one looking over your shoulder."

Until now she wouldn't have risked testing him, but she was surer of her ground now and surer of the man—a man who knew he could

swim, but dreaded the first dip of his toe in the
ocean.

She said, "Critics can be very destructive."

"Hey—" His eyebrows shot up. "Whose side
are you on, anyway?"

"I'm on the side of art and the creator." She
smiled suddenly, resisting the urge to pat him
affectionately on the cheek as she had seen his
sister do. "You may feel like running away two
minutes before we unlock the gallery door, but
you'll have a wonderful show. The critics will
be eating out of your hand." Her eyes went back
to the print on the wall. "No one could resist
work of that quality."

He stepped forward quickly and took hold of
her arms. "I'm serious about one thing," he
said. "Dead serious. Pressure means nothing to
me. If we work together you won't be able to
hurry me. I won't allow you to talk me into saving any negative that doesn't measure up, not
even if the whole show goes down the drain the
week before the opening. Do you understand
that?"

There was a strength in him she hadn't guessed
was there, and it had nothing to do with the
biting pressure of his fingers on her flesh. She
saw now that what she had taken for nervous-
ness was nothing more than the superficial flutter
of goose bumps. He was grounded solidly in who
he was and what he was able to do. She trembled

to think of what he might teach her . . . but the hunger to know was too strong to resist.

"Yes—" Her voice came out hoarsely. "Yes, I understand."

His grip tightened. "Will Remington Ware understand?"

"I'll call him." She readied herself for the kiss she sensed was coming, every nerve anticipating it. But abruptly he released her.

"I'll want to talk to him, too."

"Of course." She hid her disappointment in a show of professional efficiency. "He will expect you to speak your thoughts plainly, but I'm sure he'll agree to whatever you stipulate. He admires your work tremendously."

"Even to the extent of monopolizing his assistant for a couple of months?"

"It was his suggestion that I stay as long as I'm needed to get a show together."

"If he can uproot you whenever he wants, he must pay you very well."

Nan thought of the trip Rem had promised her and wondered why she felt guilty about not telling Spence. She knew it was none of his business. There was no reason for her to mention Davey, either. And yet she felt she should, as if his kiss had branded her, as if she belonged to him now. An absurd thought. Yet she had to bite her tongue to keep her personal business to herself.

"He pays me what I'm worth," she said.

"How can he know?" Spence answered.

She was about to give him a flip reply, when he bent his head and took the kiss that still lay waiting on her lips.

5

JOSEY AND SPENCE wanted Nan to stay on indefinitely at the Question Mark.

"Having you here would be handier," Spence said that evening at supper after their talk with Remington Ware. "We could get up every morning, gulp down our coffee and be ready for work."

"If you're worried about me," Josey put in, "don't be. I thrive on company."

"That's just it, you see." Nan was flattered by their invitation and she longed to accept it. She had never felt so at home anywhere except at her aunt's farm in Wisconsin. But she was firm in her refusal. "I *would* be company. And no matter how much you love looking after other people, Josey, there's a possibility I'll be here for two months, and that might turn even you off!"

She looked away from Spence's blue eyes boring into her. "I'll be fine at the beach cottage. The only thing that concerns me is that I can't be completely self-sufficient. You'll have to see about heating it for me, you'll have to dig me out when it snows—"

"No problem there," Spence said. "The snow doesn't get troublesome until January." His glance flicked over her. "By then we'll either have a show or we won't. In the meantime I think it's pointless for you to go off down there by yourself, when you could stay here and have Josey and me for company."

Josey's cheeks dimpled. "Maybe, brother dear, she doesn't want us for company."

Nan objected quickly, citing the cozy meal they were enjoying and the fun they'd had that morning, flushing sea gulls from the fields and bringing home a sack of newly dug potatoes from a neighboring farm.

"You don't know how much I appreciate the hospitality you've already offered me. That's why I can't impose on it. I'd hate to wear my welcome thin."

Spence eyed her evenly. "Not much chance of that."

Nan's face warmed. In Spence's studio he had held her until she broke away, flustered and alarmed by her response to his kisses.

"This won't do, you know," she had said with the little breath that was left to her. "We can't indulge in this sort of thing and get any work done."

Spence's eyes had laughed at her. "We'll set aside special breaks. We'll ring a little bell—this quarter hour for kissing, the next for making love."

Nan had resented all he was taking for granted. "You're striding ahead pretty fast, aren't you?"

The laughter moved to his lips. "Correct me if I'm wrong, but it seems to me it's you who's setting the pace."

She flushed furiously, knowing he was right. She had come too willingly into his arms. She had let her emotions have full sway, holding back nothing of what she was feeling, until the erotic beckoning of his mouth told her clearly that her response had misled him.

She forced her gaze across the supper table. "I'll try to get settled in the cottage tomorrow if you could turn on the electricity and the water for me, Spence."

"I'll come down, too," Josey volunteered, "and bring the linens and blankets you'll need."

At the neighboring farm Nan had found out more about the cottages that Spence had mentioned previously. The burly farmer's wife told Josey that her sister's family would be coming back to the island during the children's spring break and they wanted to be sure they could have the same cottage they had rented in July.

On the way back to the Question Mark, Josey had explained that the ten cottages on Malpeque Bay were their chief means of livelihood.

"We make enough off them during the tourist season," she said, "to pretty well coast the rest of the year. Of course, I have my job at the antique shop during the warm months, too, and Spence sells a painting now and then to help out, though usually what he makes off artwork is just enough to pay for his film and the rest of that developing nonsense that takes all his time."

Behind her back Spence had rolled his eyes like a bad boy properly scolded, and Nan had laughed, but in the studio after she had seen his photographs she remembered the remark and questioned him about it.

"Josey doesn't have any idea, does she, that your work is so special?"

Spence had shrugged. "She complains when I'm around, but when I'm not, I'm told she brags until she bores everybody speechless."

"Oh, I know she's proud of you. It sticks out all over her, but she really ought to understand that it's not just a hobby."

"Why?" Spence looked closely at Nan. "Why should that concern her?"

"Because," Nan spluttered, "you take your work seriously!"

"Not half as seriously as you do."

"Then you should if you don't."

"Look—" He lifted her hair off her shoulders and gathered it in his hands like a swath of silk. "Josey's world is all practicality. Cooking meals, making ends meet. She likes a pretty picture when she sees one, but it's nothing she could ever get too concerned about. It doesn't have anything to do with paying the bills and putting food on the table."

"It will have one day," Nan hotly defended. "You'll make more money off your work than Josey ever dreamed of."

"When that day comes, the money will impress her, not the composition and shadows or balance and depth in a photograph hanging in a gallery."

Nan said huffily, "She needs to be educated."

"No, she doesn't. She doesn't need anything except to marry Beau and have a houseful of children before it's too late."

Nan met Beau while they were clearing away the supper dishes. The doorbell rang and Josey brought him in to the kitchen. He was a stocky, good-looking man Josey's age, but with eyes that were older and lines around his mouth that showed he had endured suffering and resisted it, paying the price and doggedly moving ahead. Nan liked him at once.

"Beauregard Bonnell," Nan repeated when they were introduced. "What a marvelously musical name."

Beau laughed, his color rising to darken his ruddy skin. "Tell that to the foxes."

"What do you mean?"

"He means," said Josey, gazing at him fondly,

"that he's a fox farmer. That's what he does for a living."

"There aren't many of Beau's breed left on the island," Spence said. He sat down at the table and watched the smoke curl up from his friend's pipe.

"In the early 1900s," Beau began, "when my grandfather got his start, there were nearly three hundred fox ranches on the island. Then the bottom fell out of the pelt market in the thirties. A lot of people took a licking, my grandfather included. But I always liked the business. When I came back to the island a few years ago furs were making a comeback, too, so I bought some breeding stock. Things have been going pretty well ever since."

Spence smiled at Nan's wide-eyed look. "Another P.E.I. specialty for that list you're keeping."

"Fox farming," she said in a voice full of wonder. "Beau, you have a glamorous profession."

"You think so, do you?" He grinned across at her. "Come around some time and I'll show you the ninety-five percent that isn't so glamorous."

They talked for a few minutes while Josey went off to comb her hair and put on fresh lipstick, and then she and Beau went off to Alberton to the movies. Nan went into the living room, where Spence had started a fire. She picked up one of Josey's magazines.

"Did any salesgirls come knocking today?" she inquired lightly. It made her uneasy to be alone in the house with Spence, alone with the emotions he had shared earlier and her unreliable response to them. She felt too much at home here, too comfortable to keep her guard up.

He came away from the fire and sat down beside her on the sofa. "You didn't hear the blessed news on the 'Farm Hour' this morning? The campaign has concluded. Thistle Marie Thayer of Birch Hill was the high-point winner and the recipient of a superdeluxe ten-speed with dual reflectors and spacious errand basket. Three other lucky young ladies were awarded plain old bikes."

Nan smiled. "You must be terribly relieved. Now you won't have to worry when you're pulling on your underwear."

"That's a very forward remark, miss. If Josey were here, she'd take you to task."

"If Josey were here," Nan murmured, "I wouldn't have said it."

Spence laid a casual arm across her shoulder. "Does that mean we have a special rapport?"

"A little too special, I think." A note of concern entered her voice. "If we let it, it could interfere with our main objective."

"Is that why you're moving down on the beach?"

"One of the reasons." She had made up her mind during supper to tell Spence about her feelings for Davey. Her compulsive tidiness made no allowances for loose ends even in her emotional life. She was strongly attracted to Spencer Gallant...but she was still in love with Davey. When she told Spence, that would put a stop to the kisses.

But still she held back from saying Davey's name. She said instead, "What did you think of your conversation with Rem?"

"I thought he was taking a big chance with his offer. I told him so."

"I heard you. You could have put a better foot forward. Confidence is half the battle, you know. Before you got on the phone, I thought you had more than enough of that to go around. But listening to you, I wasn't so sure."

Spence shifted so that he could look directly into her eyes. "I wasn't apologizing for my work. But I'm not prolific enough to build a show on, and I haven't reached a point where I can be counted on to produce on schedule. I should have given Remington Ware a definite no." He paused. "Can you guess why I didn't?"

Nan felt a tightening in her chest. "Because it's hard to turn down a show at the Ware Gallery."

He shook his head. "It didn't cost me anything to turn it down when you mentioned it the first time. But that was before we kissed. If I'd definitely turned down Ware tonight, you'd be gone in the morning. I couldn't let that happen. Not yet."

"Spence—"

"I have to find out first what there is between us. Chemistry is one thing—" His eyes roved over her upturned face. "And you're beautiful. That accounts for a fraction of what I feel every time I look at you." His hand curved around to stroke her nape. "But what about the other two-thirds of my emotional imbalance?"

"Spence—" She found it hard to breathe with his strong steady hand massaging her neck. "Before you say anything else we need to clarify our relationship."

"At least we know it isn't love," he jested. Low laughter came from his throat. "I have a reputation for running like hell at the first hint of that entangling emotion. That's how I got to Mexico."

"If we're going to work together, Spence, you can't look at me the way you did at supper. There can't be any more innuendos and thoughts left hanging in the air and—"

"And memories of holding each other?" He pulled her against his chest with a firmly encircling arm.

"Don't, Spence—"

He dropped a kiss on her lips as gentle as spring rain, a kiss of tenderness that wasn't meant to arouse. But when he took his lips away she wanted them back again and had to knot her hands together in her lap to keep from reaching out to him.

She said in a voice thick with emotion she couldn't hide, "We have to establish some rules, Spence. You can't kiss me anytime you decide to. We can't kiss at all. We have to get a show together."

"I didn't promise Remington Ware a show. I told him I'd spend the next two months taking pictures of churches and then we'd see." The clear blue of his eyes washed over her. "I'm reserving a part of every day for finding out what we mean to each other."

"I'm not sure that's a good idea," Nan said faintly.

"Aren't you? That's not the way you're acting."

"Stop it, Spence." She freed herself and got to her feet, her gaze jumping around the room in search of diversion. "Can't we play checkers— or backgammon?" She ran an agitated hand through her silken hair. "Isn't that what people do in the evenings in isolated places? Sit by the fire and pop corn and polish their game skills?"

Spence stretched his feet out before him on the woven rug and regarded her calmly. "What's the matter?"

She turned a stricken gaze on him. "I'm trying

to be forthright and honest, and I'm not succeeding."

"Why, do you suppose?"

The quiet way he surveyed her broke down her reserve. "The chemistry you mentioned, maybe. Maybe because I like it when you kiss me, and then afterward I wish you hadn't."

"That's pretty forthright." He was silent a few seconds more and then he said, "You're interested in another man, aren't you?"

Nan trembled. "Yes."

"Somebody you're serious about?"

"We were going to get married." She moistened her lips. "But the wedding fell through."

"And you still care for the guy?"

"I'm in love with him. What broke us up was only a silly misunderstanding." She reminded herself that it was important to remember that now. Nothing had happened that couldn't be put right as soon as she got to Paris, but she mustn't get sidetracked in this out-of-the-way place just because another man's lips had briefly meant more to her than Davey's.

"We would have straightened out our problem," she said, "but he left for Europe before we had a chance."

Spence got up and poked the fire. He stood with his back to her, watching the sparks dance. "When did all this happen?"

"In April."

"A long time ago."

"Only a few months ago." Nan's heart pounded. "Do you suppose we could have a glass of wine?"

He turned around, shocking her with his careless smile. "You're not in love. You're hanging on to the shreds of something that's finished, nursing it the way you would a sore foot that you're afraid hasn't healed enough to put your weight on."

"That may be how it seems to you—" Nan began.

"That's what your kisses tell me. You should listen to them. They're saying it's time to let go, to move on to something new and better."

"Meaning an affair with you."

"Why not?" His look settled on her lips. "As you said, we have a special rapport."

Nan's gaze faltered under his penetrating stare.

"When we kiss, Nan, it isn't a commonplace occurrence." He lowered his voice possessively. "We've known each other only a short time, but I know you better than any woman I've ever taken in my arms."

"You don't know me at all," she protested. But she remembered that he had spotted the shyness in her that tightened her throat now, that made her feel naked and needing to hide from the blue-eyed stare burning into her. "Until yesterday you didn't know I existed."

"The time before I knew you doesn't seem particularly important now."

"Only because you're letting sexual attraction count for more than it ought to."

"Is that what you really think?"

She burst out suddenly, "Please—stop pressuring me!"

He went out of the room. When he came back with the wine she had asked for, she was composed again, sitting on the sofa, turning pages in her magazine.

She took the glass of sherry he handed her and watched while he set the tray and the decanter on the low coffeetable in front of them.

"Spence, I'm sorry. It isn't fair to pop into your life and turn everything upside down and then expect you to stand back as if nothing had happened."

He took a swallow of his wine. "I'm not complaining."

"Because you're generous. And because you have a sense of humor that makes it easy for you to take lightly a disappointment that's mine, not yours."

The crease deepened between his heavy brows. "Aren't you being pretty hard on me? I haven't had much experience with love, but I think I can understand what it might mean not to have it returned."

"That isn't the reason Davey and I broke up!"

" 'Davey'?" He responded to her defensiveness with a thoughtful glance. "So the beast has a name. What does he do in Europe?"

His quiet confidence unnerved her. To calm herself she sipped from her wine before she answered. "He's a photojournalist. He's a member of a select team covering the East-West talks in Paris."

She saw a flicker of something unreadable appear in Spence's eyes and she set down her glass. "What is it?"

"What's what?"

"You're hiding something."

"No—I just recalled that this morning's paper mentioned one of the conference journalists. The coincidence struck me as odd, that's all."

"Do you remember the journalist's name?" Nan sat forward on the edge of the sofa. "Was it David Pryor?"

Spence's direct look changed its focus. "It was one of those Names-in-the-News items that you glance at and forget."

"I'd like to see it." Nan's voice stretched out to a thin wire of anxiety. "Do you still have the paper?"

"It went out with the garbage after lunch." He flashed a quick smile and got up. "You said you wanted to play backgammon?"

Crossing the room, he rummaged around in a

cabinet beneath a bookshelf, talking steadily. "Just to make the game interesting, let's lay a small wager. If you win, I'll take you to dinner tomorrow night. If I win, you have to cook for me in your cottage."

"I don't enjoy cooking."

"You make a wicked icing for chocolate cake."

"I think you're lying about that newspaper article." Her fingers clutching the arm of the sofa turned icy. "Has something happened to Davey?"

Spence turned around. "What did you have in mind?"

"Snipers. Terrorists." She could barely form the words.

"It was nothing like that. I would have remembered. It would have been all over the news this evening."

He came across the room with the game board in his hand. "Are you cold? Do you want me to get your sweater?"

Nan hugged her arms closer to her breast. "I want you to tell me the truth. I can get a copy of that paper, Spence. I can go around the neighborhood until I find one, or over to Bideford. I can call a friend of Davey's that I know."

"You're getting upset about nothing."

But the misery in her face stopped anything further he might have said to lighten her mood.

Sighing, he let himself down beside her and took her cold hands in his, studying her slender fingers and their delicate oval tips.

"The man I read about can't be the same man you were in love with, Nan." His words fell on her ears with a mesmerizing softness. He waited a moment, giving her time to prepare herself. "That David Pryor," he murmured gently, "got married in Notre Dame Cathedral to an English girl."

A STORM of weeping Nan couldn't control swept over her as Spence's news sank in. All the tears that pride had held in check for so many months came pouring out. She thought of her silly hope of going to Paris and sobbed harder.

Spence leaned back against the armrest and pulled her close.

"Notre Dame Cathedral," she choked. "On ten minutes' notice, I bet. Damn Heather Bowen!"

He cradled her against his chest, smoothing her hair with light, tender strokes until her heaving shoulders finally subsided. Then he lifted her chin and put his wineglass to her lips.

"You're better now," he told her, as if saying so had made it happen and further relapses were out of the question. "Drink this."

"I'm sorry to be such a mess," she moaned. "But I hurt all over—like a truck ran over me."

"In a way, one did." He tucked her fine blond hair behind her ears and took a handkerchief out of his pocket.

"I'd better go upstairs." Nan sat up and dabbed at the swollen flesh around her eyes. "I don't want Josey and Beau to see me like this."

"They won't. They won't be back for hours."

Her face crumpled again, and he gathered her to him, slipping his arms down around her hips, easing her into his lap. "Count your blessings," he murmured. "At least you're rid of that chump."

"Davey isn't a chump." Her tears fell again. "He has an international reputation. He's always winning awards."

"He's a chump. He let you slip through his fingers. And Heather's one, too—for taking on such a smooth-headed husband."

"'Smooth-headed.'" A choked giggle mixed with Nan's sobs. "That's a term I've never heard."

"It fits him, doesn't it?" Spence brushed her wet lips with his.

"I hate him," she said, only vaguely aware that a part of her mind had turned its back on Davey. In a muffled gasp she protested, "It's only been six months. How could he have fallen in love all over again in only six months?"

Spence stayed quiet, holding her.

"I know what you're thinking," she said woe-

fully against his neck, so grateful for his comforting arms that she wanted to stay in them
forever. "You're thinking that he didn't love me.
But he did."

"Of course he did," Spence murmured.

"We disagreed, and he left in a huff and married the first woman who came along."

"That's exactly what happened, I'm sure."

They were quiet for a time after that. Spence
smoothed her arms and blotted the tears from
her cheeks.

Finally she drew a shaky breath and sat up.
"Oh, look at your shirt," she groaned, staring at
the soggy spot where her face had pressed
against his chest. "I've soaked it. I've made a
complete idiot of myself."

Spence teased, "First thing you know you'll be
calling yourself a two-headed humongous, and
I'll have to tie you up in a sack and haul you off
to the nearest zoo."

She gazed into his face, soothed in a way she
wouldn't have imagined possible a short time
before. "Dr. Gallant," she murmured, "has
anyone ever mentioned that you have a lovely
bedside manner?"

"Only the patients I take to bed."

"You have a one-track mind," she scolded,
but an insidious yearning came over her to hold
his face in her hands. She wanted to feel with
her fingertips the faint sandpapery shadow that

lay across his jaw. There was something so solid about him, something so reassuring and comforting about the easy way he looked at life's catastrophes.

In a voice too distant to be her own she asked, "Do women frequently climb into your lap and weep on your best Sunday shirt?"

"No more than one or two a week."

"Are appointments required?"

"Sometimes." He brought his lips closer. "Sometimes someone will just be standing on the porch when I open the door."

"Spence—" She swallowed. "If I'm not in love with Davey, why am I so unhappy?"

His lips moved along her cheek with a velvety softness. "There could be all kinds of reasons. Shock. Disappointment. Old dreams dying."

"Those are separate feelings, not the central one that's weighing on my heart like lead."

"That's very poetic."

"Don't make fun of me."

"That's not what I'm doing." His warm, purposeful lips with their velvety touch took her mouth...took it and withdrew in a nibbling caress, and took it again, his hunger growing past the bittersweet stain of her tears.

"You're mixed up now," he said. "You'll be all right when you've sorted out things."

She murmured in a loose, broken way, "You're so positive about everything."

"That's not so." He lay back, pulling her across his body. Her breasts yielded to the wall of his chest. She felt the outline of his thighs hardening beneath her. She felt the immense control that was holding him in check and her own fragile containment, shimmering like a soap bubble.

"Spence," she said thickly.

His lips brushed her closed eyelids. "Don't talk."

Desire drenched her, moving out through her bloodstream to every point where his body made contact with hers. "How long do you think we can lie here like this?"

His hands slid down along her hips and held them in place. "Long enough, I hope, for you to say to yourself, 'Why do I need David Pryor?' "

"I've already said it."

"Say it and mean it."

"That may take a while."

He kissed her mouth. "Then lie still, will you?"

She couldn't lie still, not with the heat rising through their clothes, mingling between them, suggesting all sorts of possibilities that quickly became physical demands.

After a minute he let her go, but when she sat up beside him she went on reacting to the churning arousal his nearness had begun. Davey had put an ache in her heart. Now added to it was another ache that Spence had started. One of his hands still lay on her hip, the fingers splayed, claiming the flesh beneath them. One word and she could put an end to this needless tension. . . .

She made herself rise. "Good night, Spence."

He came up beside her, his long body unfolding with a sensuous ease that made her heart quiver. "I'll get you settled tomorrow in your cottage."

"Are you sure you want to?" Panicked suddenly, she searched his face. "Your first decision might have been the right one, after all. Maybe in two years you'd be better prepared for a gallery show, when your direction is more certain, when—"

"When you've had time to run away and hide?"

She whispered urgently, "I like you, Spencer Gallant. I don't have a good track record. I don't know what my being here may do to your life."

"I don't know, either," he answered huskily. His eyes were darker and more penetrating than she had ever seen them. "But I'll take whatever you've brought me, Nan Blake—misery, joy. If I have to, even a long string of days wishing I'd gone to Mexico, instead."

He pulled her to him and laid his cheek on the shining crown of her head. "But I'm not sure this time if Mexico would be far enough."

6

THE COTTAGE that was to be Nan's stood scarcely a hundred yards from the sea. It perched on a ridge of sand, its row of six windows looking out toward the water. At the front door, clusters of frost-burned clover bloomed on, pinkly defiant despite the chilly morning.

Inside the cottage there was one huge room that served as kitchen, living room and sleeping gallery, with five beds in all. The only private nook in the boxlike structure was a small bedroom and a bath that opened into a larger bath with a tub and shower for general use.

Nan turned in amazement to Josey and Spence. "I could sleep a dozen people in here!"

"More than that." Josey laughed. "But you'd have to put the kids on the floor." Setting down the bundle of linens she had brought, she surveyed the room with her hands on her hips. "That's what our summer people do. They bring the whole family—the grandpas, the great-aunts. You'd think after a couple of weeks of so much togetherness they'd never want to see one another again, but the next year they can't wait to come back."

"They run each other off the road getting here," Spence agreed dryly. "It's important to have first choice of the beds."

Nan glanced away from the face that had haunted her dreams. "Which ones do you recommend?"

"In this cottage?" Josey walked around punching mattresses with authority. "I'd say this one here, and the one by the closet, and probably the single under the west window. Of course, they're all comfortable. But these are the newest. Every year we have some of the mattresses remade, but that always leaves a few at the end of the rotation that get a bit lumpy."

Spence fixed his gaze on Nan. "Which lumpy mattress do you prefer to call your own?"

"I think I'll try them all, one at a time." She glanced toward Josey, grateful for her presence. Nan's dreams had been erotic, and still clung wispily, so that just the touch of Spence's hand and the scent of his shaving lotion had unleashed a feverish yearning inside her. "Unless," she said to Josey, "you have a better suggestion."

"I have a much better one," Josey replied promptly. "Naturally you'll take the private room. Then you can close the door and pay no attention to all the people who ought to be out here snoring and aren't."

Spence laughed. "What does that mean?"

"Nan's family," Josey explained tartly. "The aunts and the nieces and the cousins she'll need to keep her company in this barny place. All these empty beds would make even a stone statue feel lonely." She turned to Nan. "Are you sure you won't change your mind and stay with us?"

"I'll be fine, Josey. You mustn't worry."

"I will, anyway. If you were with us, you wouldn't have to bother with waking up in an ice-cold house or shopping for groceries. I always cook enough for one more."

Spence cut in crisply, "Nan's made up her mind, Josey. I think we have to respect that."

Josey let out a long sigh. "I'll respect it up to a point. Try it, Nan, for a couple of days. Then if you're the least bit uneasy down here, you must come right back to the Question Mark."

"You're too good, Josey."

Josey glanced suddenly at her watch. "I'm good and late! I was supposed to be up on the road five minutes ago. Beau's passing by and picking me up."

She said to Spence, "We're going to O'Leary to talk with a fur buyer. I left lunch for you and Nan in the refrigerator. Salmon salad—and I made the moss pudding for Nan to try, but there's apple pie left if she doesn't care for it."

"Josey," Nan protested, "you have to stop fretting over me."

"She likes to fret." Spence went to the door with Josey and shooed her on her way. When he came back Nan was busy in the kitchen area putting away her store of canned goods. After watching her for a minute, he said, "What can I do to help?"

"Nothing, thanks." She was edgier, now that Josey was gone, remembering realities instead of dreams, remembering the powerful currents of sexual excitement that Spence's kiss had inspired. "I'm almost finished."

"For somebody who doesn't like to cook," he commented idly, "you bought some fancy stuff." He turned one of her purchases in his hand. "Capers?"

"For tuna-fish salad," Nan explained.

"Josey puts pickles in hers."

"So do I. But capers add an extra zest."

"You're a more enthusiastic cook than you admitted last night if you're that particular."

"I guess I exaggerated last night," Nan murmured. "Cooking was the least of my concerns."

"Does last night bother you?"

"Of course it does." She made herself meet his questioning gaze. "It's a little embarrassing having someone tell you the man you're in love with has married someone else."

Spence put aside the jar of capers and fastened his hands lightly on her shoulders. "That isn't the part of the evening I meant." Then he added quietly, "But you're not in love with David Pryor."

"Let's not discuss Davey, please."

"I think we should. You're packing around a lot of unnecessary pain."

Nan flared up suddenly. "If I am it's none of your business."

He regarded her steadily for a moment, then took his hands away. "I'll go outside and start the pump." At the door he turned around and gave her another long look. "Don't run any water until I tell you to."

Nan closed the door to the private bedroom and began putting away her clothes, but she kept an ear cocked for Spence's return. Her childish outburst shamed her. Probably it had only made Spence more certain that her feelings for Davey were on shaky ground.

But no matter what he thought he didn't deserve her snappish response. She would apologize, and then they would have to establish a new rapport—the kind of professional relationship they would have had from the start if their first meeting hadn't been so unorthodox. Her ability to handle clients was one of her greatest assets at the gallery. When artists were temperamental she knew how to set them straight without bruising their delicate egos.

She paused with one hand on the closet door.

The trouble in this case was that she was as much a part of the problem as Spence.

They were emotionally involved because of her instinctive reaction to his maleness, to his easygoing manner and the protective way he had comforted her last night.

One thing had led to another and now....

She heard the front door of the cottage open and then water singing through the lines.

Spence called out, "Turn on the tap in the bathroom."

Nan complied, trying to plan a new strategy while she waited for the water to run clear. But when she came into the main room and saw Spence standing with his hands in his pockets, staring out across the bay, she experienced once again the compelling magnetism that even the set of his shoulders conveyed.

"Spence—" Her voice caught in her throat when he turned around. "We have to talk."

He regarded her coolly. "Are you over your snit?"

"If that's what it was—yes, I'm over it." She sank down on a long studio couch that was designed to let down into still another bed. With pretended carelessness she inquired, "What's a snit, anyway?"

"A huff," he answered evenly, "of the kind you accused David Pryor of being in when he rushed out and married Heather Bowen."

"Spencer!"

"If you want to talk," he said, "let's talk. Let's not tiptoe around the big IT at the heart of our problems."

He came across the room and lowered himself into a squat little chair that brought his knees almost to his chin.

Nan said stiffly, "If we're going to speak seriously please sit somewhere else. You look ridiculous squeezed into that child's chair."

"This chair is a relic of my past. There's a part of me that has never outgrown it. If the part that has seems laughable then maybe we need to talk about that, too."

"I'm not laughing." She regarded him with tight lips. "Not about anything."

"At least you're not crying. That's progress of a sort."

"Look—I'm sorry I snapped at you about David."

"But you're still feeling as if a truck ran over you? Is that it?"

"I can't help it." She averted her gaze. "I know that for a while last night—after my crying binge—it must have seemed—you must have thought that I'd put Davey out of my mind."

If he had gauged how she felt by the signs of her arousal, what else could he think? She made herself go on. "But I could never so easily dismiss a man I had hoped to spend the rest of my life with."

He made a soft clapping sound with his hands. "Oh, nobly said, fair lady."

A flush darkened her cheeks. "I hate it when you make fun of me."

"You wouldn't mind so much if you could make fun of yourself. That's a trick you ought to learn. It smooths the sharp corners off the brickbats life throws at you."

"What would you know about that?" she asked scornfully.

"'Brickbats'?" He raised his heavy brows. "Or 'life'?"

"You don't have the remotest idea what it's like to suffer."

"I know what it's like to be jealous of a man I've never even met," he clipped out coolly. "I'm past thirty and old enough to know better. Finding out that I don't amounts to more suffering than you might imagine."

His frankness caught Nan off guard. "You're jealous of Davey?" She felt her control flying off in half a dozen directions. "Then you've mistakenly assumed there's more between us than there actually is."

"There seems to be enough to have kept me awake most of last night." He got up and ambled toward her. "If I'm not careful, I might even fall in love with you."

Above her pounding heart she tried to match the teasing quality in his tone. "You're reading too much into a couple of kisses."

"Am I?" He stood over her. "I'm not in this by myself, you know. You care about me, too."

"I care about you—of course I do. I've already said so." Blood rushed to her cheeks. "I've also amply demonstrated—too amply, it seems—that I'm physically attracted to you. But I'm not mistaking attraction for love."

"You claim to have been in love with David Pryor. Wasn't he physically attractive?"

"You're deliberately mixing everything up!"

"A natural consequence of dealing with a mixed-up lady." His hands encircling her waist drew her to him with a tantalizing slowness. "Why do you think sexual attraction exists if it isn't meant to bring two people together?"

Nan's voice wavered. "What I'm saying is that sex and love can't be equated."

"Oh, I'll agree to that. One," he said huskily, "leads to the other." Then he bent his head and brought his lips to hers.

A new intensity in his kiss, a rough, unbridled urgency, startled her and made her try to draw back. But the compelling circle of his arms refused to let her go.

Her breathing quickened as his ardor increased. The determined questing of his mouth brought vividly to the fore a host of untapped powers that clamored to be set free. All that was female within her sizzled in response to his hand at her breast, provocatively kneading. . .exploring. . . . An alarming sensation attacked the back of her knees and pooled out into her bloodstream.

"Spence—" she gasped when she was finally able to tear her mouth away. But the desire he had aroused continued to pour through her. The heated insistence of his caresses had involved all of her, from the electric tremor that sped up her spine to the spreading weakness in her lower body.

"Sex and love may lead to each other," she told him in a desperate whisper, "but not in that order—not for me."

His heavy-lidded gaze refused to take her protest seriously. "You weren't noticeably reluctant a minute ago."

Scarlet stained her cheeks. "It took a minute to realize that more was involved than a passionate kiss." She floundered for a reason that would excuse her unbridled response. "You were holding me, but you were acting out of your resentment of Davey."

"If I was," he answered evenly, "the resentment was subconscious, and definitely secondary." He fixed a look of naked desire on her. "I want you—and it's no good pretending that you don't want me."

His raw directness rocked her as he went on hoarsely, "You can only postpone the inevitable, Nan. You can't deny forever the pressure that's building between us."

She knew he was right. Even as she struggled to free herself from his embrace her subliminal urges had gone on responding to his touch and to the current that ran just beneath his overt sexuality. The powerful mixture of male strength and tenderness that had first attracted her blocked out memories of Davey's caresses as if they had never existed.

Abruptly he challenged her again. "So where do we go from here?"

"I know where I ought to go—" Nan fought the urge to return to his arms. "Back to Boston."

"You'd run away?" Ignoring her resistance, he gathered her to him once more. "Is that how you operate—you strike a crippling blow and flee to the hills?"

"I came here to help you set up a show," she sighed. "How can I do that now?"

"Why can't you? What's stopping you?"

"You, this—" Her heart thudded painfully against his chest. "Even if we start out half a room apart we end up in each other's arms."

"I've noticed that." His low, murmuring breath stirred the wisps of hair that curled at her temples. "And I don't object. Why are you objecting?"

She called herself back from the dizzying heights toward which he was leading her. "Because—" she began, pulling a long, quivering breath up from her lungs and freeing herself.

"Whenever you hold me, I lose my perspective—and because no matter how many times you may deny it, I did love David Pryor."

She made herself meet Spence's insistent gaze. "I made an emotional error, falling in love with Davey, and I have to come to terms with it. I have to stake out my priorities all over again and refocus my directions." Misery etched itself across her face. "I can't do that if I'm having an affair with you."

While she talked, his look softened. With a delicate touch he traced her cheekbone. "An 'affair,'" he said. "That's too flimsy a word to explain what I want to share with you." The penetrating blue of his eyes took hold of her. "Something brought us together besides the Ware Gallery, Nan. We have an affinity that enables you to inhibit my natural impulse to run when the violins start playing. It enables me to spot that shy self in you that no one else has ever explored." He lowered his voice to a husky whisper. "That shyness is mine, Nan. It's been waiting all the years of your life for me to claim it."

He went on in the silence that shut them off even from the pounding surf. "I don't know when it was decided—or where or by whom—but you and I have a commitment to each other. When we make love—and we will—we'll be honoring it."

His words washed over her with the same

overwhelming power that his rugged virility communicated to all that was female within her. With all her heart she yearned to take what he was offering and to give back the full range of her own offering. But two warring forces held her in check: the painful specter of a would-be marriage that had blown away in the wind and a professional reluctance to jeopardize Remington Ware's trust.

Spence watched her for a moment and then turned away. She heard him behind her, opening cabinets, locating the coffeepot finally and filling it. While it made its cheerful perking noises, he stood staring through the front windows at a bank of clouds building on the horizon.

Nan sank into the couch, her hands gripped in her lap, all her senses raw but alert. Only a few events in her lifetime had engraved themselves in every detail on her brain. Parting with David was one of them. This was another. No matter what happened, she knew she would remember forever the miniature pots of red geraniums printed on the curtains framing Spence's dark head. For the rest of her days, the *chip*, *chip*, *chip* of a sparrow on the doorstep would recall it.

He brought the coffee in two steaming mugs and sat down beside her. "Answer this," he began bluntly. "Do you want to stay?"

Her ragged voice challenged him. "That's beside the point, isn't it?"

"It's the whole point. You have to decide what matters and what doesn't."

"Your show matters."

"If you go away, you can forget the show." He shook his head, forestalling any objections. "That's not a threat. I'm just reminding you of how I am. One morning I'll wake up with the urge to carve or to search out an Acadian ancestor and that's what I'll do. I may not think of photographing churches again for another six months."

Nan's eyes searched his face. "If I stay, do you think I can change that? Are you sure if I could that you'd want me to?"

He considered her question for a minute that seemed to stretch to an hour. At last he said, "I'm sure I want you here. We'll work it out from there."

The seductive spell his words cast settled over her forebodingly. *I should get up*, she thought dimly. *I should leave now, while we still possess our separate lives, our separate goals.* But her legs refused to move; her tongue refused to say goodbye.

At last agreement rasped from her parched throat. "I want to stay, Spence, but I have to do a good job for the gallery. I'm obligated to my career, to Rem's trust in me. You have to understand that."

He nodded.

"If we're going to work together successfully we'll have to establish some guidelines." She felt the warmth of his hands sliding up from her wrists, moving in behind her nape to clasp the white stalk of her neck. "We can't always be touching," she warned faintly. "We can't always be kissing. Do you promise, Spence?"

"I promise." His lips moved persuasively at the corner of her mouth. "Starting tomorrow."

7

GOING OUT WITH SPENCE each day to view the island's churches proved to be even more of an endurance test than Nan had feared.

Spence, however, broke no rules. After the morning he persuaded her to stay, he had, at her request, kept to a minimum the evenings he asked her out. True to his promise, there was never the slightest suggestion that he might take her in his arms when they were working. But he knew how to make the most of a look or to comment quietly on the flattering color of a sweater or the perfume she was wearing. Moving along at her side, he still kept a distance by means of the detached air of an artist absorbed in his subject. But with a deadly accuracy he sensed all her moods, and knew when her attraction to him was least guarded.

Each day was torture. After the evenings they did go out together, there were wispy remembrances of being held next to his wide chest or of long, lingering looks across candlelit dining tables.

Worse were the grating memories of the
nights she spent by herself, trying to do the
paperwork for two upcoming gallery shows but
feeling lonelier than she could ever remember
being. Sometimes Spence explained how he
spent his time away from her—working in his
darkroom, painting, carving. Sometimes he
gave no explanations, and she was left to
speculate on where he might have been and
whom he might have been with.

Daily as they drove around the countryside
with the car heater going, Spence's warmed skin
seemed to take on the smells of summer—of sun
and wave-kissed breezes and crushed grass
underfoot. Nan could imagine long, lazy days
lying in the sand with him...moonlight
swims...picnics in grassy meadows. Beneath
his Windbreaker the solid set of his shoulders
was a nagging reminder of his arms sliding
around her and the potency of his embrace.
Covert glances at his profile awoke anew memories of his lips on hers and left her limp with
longing.

Her dreams of David Pryor had stopped altogether. Spence was the only man she thought of
now, awake or sleeping. She found it increasingly difficult to hold in check her need to ex-
plore the erotic imaginings his nearness evoked.
She managed only by keeping fresh the raw
uncertainty left over from Davey's betrayal.

Repeatedly she warned herself that what she was feeling for Spence could be a backlash.

She lectured herself frequently on the conflict of personalities that existed between her and Spence. Nothing lasting could develop between two people who viewed life so differently. Spence was too easygoing, too willing to find contentment in the island's backwaters, while the real excitement of the art world was taking place in the bustling cities he mocked her for missing. The slow-moving pace of the island appeared to offer all the creative stimulus he needed. Sometimes, watching him, fascinated by his work, it seemed enough for her, too.

But most days left her feeling exhausted from the gnawing turmoil inside her and unfulfilled. Her saving grace was the one thing she had learned during the numbing weeks after her breakup with Davey: that it was possible to go on functioning professionally even when the rest of one's life was in tatters...or even, she was beginning to realize, when one was falling in love again and there seemed no way at all to stop.

By THE END of the third week, trailing after Spence through St. John the Baptist Church in Miscouche, Nan marveled at how much they had accomplished in spite of her distress.

Early on, at her insistence, they had organized

their work into systematically photographing and cataloging the island's churches, county by county.

Spence had objected at first to changing his usual haphazard methods. "That's the way I like to do things," he complained, and for a few days Nan let it go.

But one morning, after watching him shoot a whole roll of film on a single structure that he blithely dismissed afterward as too Gothic for his tastes, she concluded that they couldn't possibly make their January deadline if he went on indulging himself in the freedom he was accustomed to. Tactfully she approached him with a more practical way to proceed.

"Assuming that you're going to do the show," she began carefully, "we ought to give some thought to working toward certain preconceived dates."

She saw the scowl that crossed his face and went on in an easier tone. "It needn't be anything to worry about, but there's no harm in making a few plans. I think you'll see how painless a schedule can be if you'll try restricting yourself to a couple of identifying shots at each stop—nothing artistic or time-consuming. From those, I'll put together a file of what we have to work with. Then you can study the prints and pick out the churches you want to do seriously. You won't use film unnecessarily, and we won't waste precious days taking pictures you'll never need."

Spence agreed reluctantly, but later in the day he made an offhand comment that upset her. "I hadn't realized you were such a businesswoman. I never would have imagined there was so much logic and precision in that blond head."

"Why not?" In Boston she had valued her concise way of dealing with management problems. She owed her job to it, in fact. She felt affronted.

"Logic and precision," Spence answered, "are all angles and straight lines. All cubicles and locked boxes." His gaze drifted over her, so tangibly erotic it made her tremble. "Logic is dry...it's sterile." He paused, still looking at her. "When I think of you I think of softness and shimmer and deep wells of understanding."

Then he walked off, leaving her frustrated and speechless. She didn't see him that evening, and the following day she felt self-conscious in his presence, as if she had deliberately failed him and lost ground in his estimation. By evening her restraint with him passed, however, and when Spence kissed her good-night after dinner in Summerside, her softness and shimmer appeared to be all that was needed to inspire his ardor. She had to tear herself from his embrace, before she gave in to the growing need inside her that had nothing at all to do with logic and precision.

This day in Miscouche, however, Nan quickly

left off thinking of their personal predicament. Following Spence around the great church, she sensed a new restlessness in him. His lack of interest in the towering edifice that was the island's most photographed religious building alerted her professional intuition, and at once she turned her skills toward drawing him out.

"It's too elegant, isn't it?" she commented as they were leaving. "It's like the others we've seen this morning—impressive and historically significant, but lacking the exciting primitive qualities of the starker simpler buildings."

She was thinking in particular of the two they had seen the day before. They had thrilled her even though they had disrupted the orderly plan she had prescribed for Spence.

The first was in the far reaches of Prince County, near Tignish. They had come upon it in a morning mist, and disregarding the business-like approach he had been obediently adhering to, Spence had leaped from the car and gone running toward it. For the next hour she hadn't been able to budge him—though admittedly she hadn't really tried.

According to their schedule they were due in Bloomfield at ten, with four more stops before lunch. But the various phases of altering light on the tiny old building were fascinating to her, too, and she didn't blame Spence for lingering—then or later, when he halted again before a similar structure of gaunt lines and capricious gingerbread. Enchanted, she watched him spend another hour photographing from every angle the play of maple shadows on its pristine whiteness.

It was the first time she had seen him fully engaged in executing his talents, and the experience was thrilling. He knew exactly what he wanted, and he went after it to the exclusion of everything else, including her. But she hadn't minded. If it hadn't been for the January deadline looming ahead she would have been happy to sit there forever, admiring Spence at his work.

Now, standing outside St. John the Baptist Church, he said, "A primitive expression is what the focus of the collection is narrowing down to."

He opened the car door for her and looked back at the pride of Miscouche in its spacious setting. "Churches like this are intriguing in their own way, but they won't fit in with what I've decided the show at the gallery should say."

Nan was too excited to speak. Half believing that she was whistling in the dark, she had been telling herself for days that he was going to do the show, but this was the first solid declaration he had made.

Breathlessly she waited for him to come around the car and slide behind the wheel. Then she burst out, "That's why you're not photographing this morning for the files, isn't it?"

The files were only two-thirds complete, and earlier she had been annoyed by his balky resistance to take the usual shots. Now her irritation vanished as excitement took its place. "You've settled on a theme!"

He nodded. Turning the car around, he headed it back toward Lady Slipper Drive. "At Tignish yesterday and at the church in the maple grove afterward the whole thing started coming together in my mind."

"Have you already made the prints?"

"Last night." He flashed his first boyish grin of the morning. "They're perfect, Nan. They capture exactly the elusiveness I've been feeling but haven't been able to catch on film."

Because she had restricted him too much? What if she had stifled this lovely moment right out of existence? The thought was too depressing to contemplate, and she brushed it aside with an eager question. "When can I see them?"

"Come to the house for dinner tonight."

Nan hesitated. The Question Mark more than any other place on the island fostered a feeling of intimacy they both found difficult to resist. She made her visits there as brief and as far between as possible. "I'm dying to see them," she said, "but I'll wait till tomorrow."

She knew he understood why she was hedging, but he pressured her, anyway, his gaze as deliberate as his question. "What's the harm in coming to dinner?"

He stopped the car again in front of a small café that advertised, on a cheerful hand-printed sign stuck in the window, home fries and hamburgers. Swinging around in the seat, he pressed her further. "Josey misses you, and so do I."

"Josey fixed lunch for me last week and you see me everyday."

"It isn't the same thing."

The solitary ache inside her affirmed that he was right. When he let her out after work and left her to putter around the cottage and listen to the waves smashing on the shore, she hungered for the closeness they enjoyed when they were together: for his arms around her, a low fire on the hearth and the steady ticking of the clock.

A burst of laughter from two men emerging from the café reminded her that a question still hung between them, unanswered.

She made her decision quickly. "I won't come for dinner tonight," she told him. "I have a couple of business calls to make. But tell Josey if she isn't busy tomorrow I'll run over for a chat while you're in Summerside doing your shopping."

The Gallants were attending a wedding soon. The son of an old family friend was marrying in

Charlottetown, and Josey had made it clear during Nan's last visit that Spence was going to have
a new suit for the occasion.

Spence's response had been less than enthusiastic. "I have a fine suit I can wear—my old
gray flannel."

"It's old all right!" Josey had spent the next
ten minutes berating that favored outfit from
Spence's wardrobe. "The lapels are wrong, the
buttons are wrong—"

Finally she pinned him down to a specific day
and lined him up with a tailor in Summerside.
Spence had promised to be there at three on Wed-
nesday—tomorrow.

He made no reply to her refusal to come to dinner, and she got out of the car and followed him
in a matching silence into the restaurant.

When he had found a place for them and sat
down across from her in the narrow booth, she
tried to revive his enthusiasm about doing the
gallery show.

"I can't tell you, Spence, how pleased I am that
you've made up your mind to go ahead with the
collection."

He ordered for them and then gave her a long
look as the waitress walked away. "If words fail
you," he commented dryly, "try telling me with a
kiss."

"'A kiss!'" She laughed in surprise, feeling
protected enough in the crowded room to joke.

"Here? Would you want me to kiss you in front of all these people?"

"Normally, no. But when kisses are rationed. . . ." He let the words die, his eyes darkening suddenly. "I'm tired of what we're doing to each other, Nan."

"Spence—" Without any warning he had ripped apart the fragile facade that had made it possible for them to function over the past few weeks. Hurriedly she urged, "Don't upset things now. We've been getting along so well."

"Have we?" His eyes stayed on her, wedging into her with their blueness. "We've been like dinosaurs walking on eggs. That's not getting along. That's maintaining the status quo. Boring under any circumstances, pure hell in this case."

"We agreed—"

"The contract is about to expire."

"Because you're suddenly tired of it?"

"Because of what it's doing to us. Because of what we're ignoring. Letting time be swallowed up while we turn our backs on what really concerns us."

Nan thought wildly of what a strange place he had chosen to bare their darkest secrets. How was she to deal with him when every fiber in her body wanted him, needed him, and every cell in her brain told her they were mismatched in every way except the physical?

"I know it's been difficult," she began, yielding

suddenly to a strange surge of weightlessness
that came from her heart, an impulse urging her
to be honest, to be tender. Maybe Spence was
right, an inner voice said. Maybe the time had
come to take whatever risks her growing love required. Maybe she was brave enough now to
open herself again to the possibility of pain and
disillusionment—a small price to pay for fulfillment, if that was what Spence was offering.

Opening her mouth to pour out her heart, she
realized she no longer had his attention. He was
gazing past her to the other side of the room
where the entrance was.

"It's Cate," he said when he saw Nan's startled
look.

"Who?" Nan turned her head.

"Catherine Donohue. An old friend. She's
Josey's boss at the antique shop."

Cate. Yes. Josey had spoken of her. Nan
picked out the woman, attractive in a tweed
blazer and cream-colored skirt. She was a few
years older than Nan but about the same height,
with the same coloring and a vibrant, easy grace
much like Nan's, as she moved into the room.
Brown hair curled around her angular face and
bright brown eyes, as bold as Nan's, warmed as
she spotted Spence and raised a hand in greeting.

He looked at Nan. "Shall I ask her to join us?"

"Yes, of course." Feeling disoriented and cut
off from the confession she had been about to

spill out to Spence, Nan watched his lanky frame unfold, and then with a light-fingered fear tripping over her skin she followed his quick steps across the crowded restaurant.

Cate, her brain said again. The fears she had imagined in her loneliest hours at the cottage had a name now and a face—a lovely face, she saw as Spence brought her back to the booth, guiding her with a familiar hand at her elbow. He looked pleased. Pleased and comfortable. Nan realized with a sickening certainty that this was a woman Spence knew well...one he saw frequently...and one who was as interested in him as he seemed in her.

Cate smiled disarmingly as she settled across from Nan after Spence's introduction.

"Spence and Josey have so much to say about you these days—" she told Nan "all raves, of course—that I've started thinking of you as a myth." She sent an amused glance toward the steaming bowl the waitress was setting down in front of Nan. "It's reassuring to discover that you're real enough to enjoy vegetable soup and plain-old crackers in a place as ordinary as this."

Spence laughed and sat down beside her. "Nan likes moss pudding, too."

"Josey's moss pudding?" Cate shrugged. "Who wouldn't like it—or anything else Josey cooks." Turning back to Nan, she said, "Isn't she marvelous in the kitchen?"

"Too marvelous," Nan agreed, so tense she wondered if she might snap in two. "I had to move out while I could still get into my clothes."

Cate laughed and changed the subject. "I'm fascinated that Spence's photographs may show in Boston. Josey told me how Mr. Ware became acquainted with his work. How are things going?"

They chatted for a few minutes. Spence and Nan waited with their own soup until Cate's arrived. Gradually Nan felt herself relaxing. Cate was so genuinely interested in all they had been doing and so warmly enthusiastic that it was impossible not to like her.

When the soup came, Nan said, "It's been so exciting watching the preliminaries shape up. But it's Spence who should be giving you the details." She glanced at him and saw he was looking at them both with a faint smile on his lips. Her stomach knotted again. Perhaps he had already confided the details.

"In the end," Nan said more guardedly, "what the show amounts to will be up to him."

"Ah." Cate nodded. "Of course. I understand. But you're the guiding hand that will get him there, aren't you?"

Nan flushed. Had Spence complained that her hand was too insistent? "I organize. I make suggestions. But no one knows better than I do that I'm not the artist. I have no talent in that area at all."

Cate insisted. "You have an excellent eye, I'm told."

Not told by Josey. Josey wouldn't know. Nan's heart pounded. How many evenings while she was pacing the cottage had Spence held Cate, kissed her as he kissed Nan herself, obliterating everything except the rapture his lips could arouse?

It took all of Nan's will to steady her voice. "I've been fortunate enough to acquire exposure to excellent work at the gallery. Experience is everything—as I'm sure you know from your own work." She picked up the soupspoon and set it down again when she saw she was trembling. "By the way, have the police caught your burglars?"

Cate's look showed surprise that Nan was so knowledgeable about her own affairs. Spence explained. "Nan got snared into helping me with a cake the day Josey went over to do inventory after the break-in. That was her introduction to P.E.I.'s crime circuit."

"I see." Cate smiled. "Well, nothing has been recovered yet—which has my insurance company agonizing. But there's hope that an arrest will be made soon."

To Nan's relief the focus of attention shifted to Cate. While they ate she entertained them with an account of the progress the island police had made in tracking down the goods taken from her shop. She was too open and friendly to find fault with, and Nan was sure that if they had met under different circumstances they would have become fast friends. But she wasn't sorry when the meal was over.

When she and Spence were in his car again, waving as Cate drove off, a tiny sigh of relief escaped her.

The corners of Spence's mouth twisted in a suppressed smile. "Didn't you enjoy your lunch? Or is it Cate you didn't enjoy?"

"Cate was charming." Nan eyed him coolly. "But I thought it was interesting that out of all the restaurants on the island she happened to pick this one."

Moving the car back onto the road, Spence agreed. "I often stop at this café, but I've never seen Cate here before—" he paused to grin "—believe it or not."

Nan pretended a keen interest in a plump bird on a telephone wire. "Maybe she came looking for you."

"If she had, she would have said so. Cate," he said pointedly, "isn't one to beat around the bush."

Nan's temper flared. "Neither am I," she retorted. "If you didn't invite her to meet us there, then she saw your car and came in to see what I was like."

His brows lifted. "What do you think her opinion was?"

Nan put a tart end to the conversation. "I hope she liked me as much as I liked her."

They rode along in a strained silence after that, each one absorbed in his or her own thoughts. But when Spence turned off onto a bumpy road leading toward the coast, Nan came to attention and glanced around.

"Is there a church down here?"

"No, only Bedeque Bay, and the strait beyond."

Stopping the car atop one of the sandstone cliffs that rimmed the shore, he climbed out, inquiring over his shoulder, "Do you want to come along down to the beach?"

Nan wondered what he expected her to do if she didn't. The mild carelessness of the invitation was in sharp contrast to Spence's intensity toward her just before Cate had joined them. Her appearance, Nan thought bitterly, had jarred everything else out of his head.

Feigning an indifference to match his, Nan climbed out of the car. At once the view enthralled her. The strait was like glass, and so blue it was hard to differentiate between water and sky. A slow-moving ferry poking across it seemed to be painted in a pale wash of watercolors.

Then as she stepped out to the edge of the cliff a sudden whipping wind sprang up, tossing her hair and twisting the smoke on a distant freighter.

Picking her way down toward the shore, she missed Spence's guiding hand at her elbow and thought of it wrapped protectively around Cate's. The wind swirled, tearing at her clothes, and her pleasure in the view lessened. When they were once more on level ground she said with a testiness she despised but couldn't control, "I could have broken my neck back there. You don't have to take quite so literally the hands-off edict."

"Oh, I see." He put his camera down on a loaf-shaped rock and regarded her from beneath his heavy brows. "The rules are flexible as long as it's you who's bending them. Maybe you'd better list them and give me a copy. Then we'll both know where I stand."

She passed coolly by him. "Where I'd like for you to stand is as far from me as possible."

She heard his amused chuckle, and then in a change of mood too swift for her to comprehend he spoke commandingly at her back. "Nan—"

She turned defiantly into the face of his camera. The shutter clicked.

A stab of surprised pleasure replaced her annoyance. "You didn't tell me you were going to do that."

"I didn't want you posing." He photographed her twice more in rapid succession, talking while he worked. "You don't object, do you?"

"Of course not." She was sure he could see the

excitement she felt. "I wasn't prepared, that's all."

He hadn't mentioned photographing her since the first day they'd met. She thought he had dismissed the idea, but now it wasn't the sea or the cliffs or Cate that engrossed him, but her! In spite of her delight she couldn't suppress an instinctive regret. "I only wish I weren't quite so windblown."

Suddenly he was annoyed. "Do you think I give a damn how your hair looks? Walk over there. Look out at the water."

She respected the authority in his voice, humbled because of her enormous regard for his talent and flattered, too. But a prickle of disappointment at the way he was directing her pecked at her in spite of her pleasure.

He continued to bark out orders for another few minutes. Finally, in a state of jittery self-consciousness, she said, "Are you nearly finished?"

His answer came back curtly. "I'll tell you when I'm finished." Kneeling on the sand, he slanted the camera toward her face. "Turn your head slowly, left to right. Stop when you're looking straight at me—*stop*, I said!"

There was another fast succession of clicks, and then he got to his feet, brushing the sand from his knees. "There." For the first time since he had begun, he looked at her as if he saw her. "That wasn't so awful, was it?"

Instantly she forgave him for his irritable treatment of her. "It wasn't awful at all."

Her sudden shyness would ordinarily have aroused intimate comments, but this time he said instead, "Thanks for that wicked scowl at the end. That's just the sort of thing I wanted on my film."

"I see." She did see—with depressing clarity. He had deliberately provoked her. As a skilled associate of the Ware Gallery, she had to commend his creative wizardry; he was a master of his craft. But as a woman, she ached to be told that he had photographed her because she was beautiful and desirable. . .and that he loved her beyond all reason. . . .

"Raw emotions are genuine," he went on, "and rare. Come on," he said without looking at her again. "I'll take you home."

8

THE NEXT AFTERNOON, in the cozy Question Mark kitchen, Josey served coffee and tiny strawberry tarts with dollops of whipped cream swirled on top. During the night, while Nan had tossed restlessly, winter had arrived. The blustery wind had blown away the golden autumn days the countryside had enjoyed for a week and now rain was tapping on the windowpanes and making a blur of the duck pond in the meadow.

Josey rocked comfortably and sipped from her cup. "So you've met Cate," she said at the end of a long, quiet minute.

Nan nodded. "Yesterday. At a café." She shoved to the back of her mind the scene that had followed and the beach scene afterward. "Spence told you, I guess, how we happened to run into her."

"Actually, it was Cate who mentioned it." Josey paused to stir her coffee. "She came over to go with Spence this afternoon to help him pick out the fabric for his suit."

"Oh, I see." Nan's fingernails dug into the arms of the chair. "Well—" The clock bonged the hour, giving her a moment to collect herself. "I'm sure he'll welcome a female point of view."

Josey made a wry face. "Thank heaven it didn't have to be mine. I can't bear to shop with Spence. He looks at this and he looks at that, until you think you'll go mad—and then he comes away without buying a thing. I told Cate that if he behaves that way today not to let him come home."

"Cate and Spence—" Nan tried to find enough moisture inside her mouth to finish her sentence. "They're good friends, aren't they?"

"They're quite a bit more than that." Josey smiled and dipped into her mending basket to pull out a brown sock. "Any day now I expect they'll be announcing that they're getting married."

A lump as large as a tart blocked Nan's breathing. She licked her lips and tried to calm her whirling thoughts. "Are they making plans?"

Josey answered, "Privately I'm sure they are. I know he's seeing her lots more than he did for a while. Of course that was mostly during the tourist season." Her sigh came out reminiscently weary. "We hardly have time to breathe when the tourists are here. There's always something to tend to at the cottages and Cate has her shop to keep her busy till all hours."

Nan remarked woodenly, "The shop keeps you busy, too." But her thoughts were reeling. Spence and Cate were on the brink of marriage. All the signs were there, of course—the evenings when Spence didn't show up at the cottage, Cate's not-too-subtle appearance at the café.... It had been easier to pretend while they sat there spooning soup that there was nothing serious in their relationship, easier to put off facing reality. Now it was Heather and Davey all over again, and inside her chest, her heart was turning to stone.

Oblivious to Nan's sudden pallor, Josey carried on with her comfortable chatter. "I don't take time to cook in the summer, I can tell you that. It's sandwiches till they run out of our ears. Of course, I have to can the fruits and vegetables as they come in, and I do some freezing. The strawberries in these tarts arrived from King's County one day and I was washing and hulling them until two in the morning. We had such a rush of customers at the shop right at closing time. Then, when I finally did get home, a family on the beach was moving out and another moving in—"

As Josey talked, Nan's glazed stare followed her shiny needle in and out of the toe of the sock. But her thoughts were in Summerside.

Were Spence and Cate sharing a drink some-where? Sharing a kiss? A shiver ran over her as she imagined Spence stroking Cate's creamy flesh...tangling his fingers in her soft brown curls....

Josey broke in with a question. "How much cooking are you doing at the cottage?"

"'Cooking'?" Nan started. "Oh, just enough to get by. I'm not very good at it, I'm afraid."

"You should have stayed here with us and let me look out for you. Like what I was telling Cate—"

"Josey—" Nan clenched her fingers in her lap. One more word about Cate and she'd scream. "Have I interfered with anything, coming over here this afternoon? Are you expecting Beau?"

"'Beau'!" Josey laughed. "You don't know what a man of routine he is, do you? The foxes get all his daytime attention. Anytime he shows up here before seven in the evening it's some-thing out of the ordinary. You can set your watch by Beau."

"It must be nice to have a man you can count on," Nan murmured.

Josey laid down her sewing. "I'll bet in Boston you have half a dozen men knocking on your door."

Nan smiled feebly. "Just one as attentive as Beau would be enough." But it would never be Spence. "Actually," she said, more for her own benefit than Josey's, "I really don't have time for men."

Josey nodded. "I can understand that. Years ago Beau asked me to marry him, but I was busy, too. So he married Alice Jane Hamilton, instead." She pursed her lips in a way that made her look five years older. "They weren't happy. Maybe that was my fault. I can't say. I can't help it if it was. I had other responsibilities."

She gazed thoughtfully at Nan. "The one thing I can't help worrying about is that it might be happening all over again."

Nan closed her mind to what might be happening in Summerside. "What do you mean, Josey?"

Josey shrugged. "You've probably figured out that Beau still wants me to marry him. I hope someday I can. But I won't consider it, of course, until I know that Spence is settled."

"What does Spence have to do with it?"

"Everything," Josey answered. "I would have married Beau after papa died, but I couldn't leave Spence."

Nan sat forward in her chair. "You can't mean that, Josey!" Nan's own problems flew out of her head. "Spence would never tie you down."

Josey agreed. "I guess you could say it was me who tied myself down. But I couldn't go waltzing off to make a home for Beau and me when this is all the home Spence has."

"This happens to be a very nice home!" Nan spluttered. "Spence is a grown man. He can look out for himself."

Josey smiled. "Can he really? He can't even ice a cake without bringing in help the first time the doorbell rings."

"Who says he has to have icing on his cake, for heaven's sake? Or cake at all!" Nan's indignation mounted. "What makes you think Spence is so delicate that you have to renounce your happiness with Beau to keep him comfortable and waited on?"

Josey blinked. "I don't *have* to. I'm doing it because I care about my brother."

"More than you care about Beau?"

"In a different way, Nan, entailing different responsibilities." The strained note in her voice let Nan know that if she had a brother herself she might understand.

"It seems to me that if you love a man enough to want to marry him, he ought to come first in your life, before anything else."

Josey withdrew to her darning. "There's more coffee on the stove."

Nan ignored the warning. "Isn't that what the marriage ceremony says?" she persisted. " 'Forsaking all others'?"

"When Spence gets settled, I'll get married. May I bring you another tart?"

Nan's lips tightened. "No, thank you."

They sat on for a minute in a stiff silence, listening to the rain. Finally Nan pulled in her breath. "I'm sorry, Josey. I realize I don't know you well enough to bluster around about the way you're running your life, but it seems such a *waste* to me. You and Beau have loved each other for so long—"

"Let's not discuss it, if you don't mind."

"I wouldn't have said anything at all," Nan protested, "except that I was trying to shed a little light on a subject you claimed was troubling you."

"I'm more troubled now," Josey replied in a starchy voice, "than I was to begin with."

"Then I'm terribly sorry." Nan got out of her chair, feeling as if the ceiling had caved in. "Please forget everything I said. All I wanted to do was help, Josey. You're a wonderful woman. You deserve to be happy with Beau in a home of your own."

"You don't care if Spence is happy, do you?" Josey said thinly. She fixed her gaze on Nan's astonished face. "And to think I once wished he'd fallen in love with you, instead of Cate."

Nan stared, speechless.

"Oh, yes, I did wish that. I even went so far as to say a few prayers about it. I guess that makes me as big a fool as you think I am."

Nan turned away, blinded by tears of wrenching regret. "I don't think you're a fool at all," she choked out as she started toward the door. "I think you're too kind for your own good— and for everyone else's."

9

WHEN SPENCE ARRIVED at his usual time the next morning, Nan was busy at her makeshift desk in the kitchen alcove.

"I'm not going with you," she announced without looking up.

"Why?" He shut the door and came across the room. "Because we exchanged a few harsh words day before yesterday?"

"Because I may be coming down with a cold." She let him see her tear-swollen eyelids as proof. "Anyway, you don't need me."

Leaning on the bar, he pinched a corner off the breakfast roll she had pushed aside and popped it into his mouth. "Who says I don't need you?"

"We're finished with the photos for the file. My going along this morning won't serve any purpose."

His tone changed to a softly persuasive murmur. "You serve a purpose just by being you."

Nan brought up her guard. With a simple wheedling phrase he thought he could turn her resolve to jelly. But she was through making a fool of herself in front of the Gallants.

"Please don't be difficult, Spence. I need to stay by the phone in case Rem calls. We've scheduled other shows besides yours, you know. One of them is opening next week."

"Opening in Boston," he persisted. "You're here."

"I'm expected to offer suggestions wherever I am." She got very busy searching through the red notebook she called her "gallery bible." "I've told you before that I have certain responsibilities that have to be fulfilled."

"You told me that you were free until Christmas to do whatever was needed here."

"I can't be much more help to you until you have something ready for the gallery show."

"I do have." He tossed a brown envelope down in front of her. "Have you forgotten the church near Tignish? And the one in the maple grove?"

Remorse swept her mind clear of everything except her failed obligation to Spence. Lost in her own troubles, she had blocked out what was supposed to be her principal concern here— Spence's work.

Reaching hastily for the envelope, she pulled out the top print. The Tignish church sprang up at her from its icy knoll like a lovely bride veiled in mist. All the excitement of watching Spence photograph it came back to her as she gazed at the intricate patterns of moisture detailed on the windows and the "diamonds" sparkling from the gables. In the eerie incandescent light of dawning, the building's sharp corners were gently softened, the gingerbread trim appeared as delicate as old lace.

Nan looked up with shining eyes. "Oh, Spence!"

"Like it?"

Awe was in every hushed syllable that fell from her lips. "I can't begin to tell you how much."

"Look at the next one," he directed.

Eagerly she pulled it out. It was the church in the maple grove, and like the first photograph, a masterpiece. Golden sunlight defined the rectangular building and showed with compelling sharpness the perfectly focused leaf shadows that lay across its face. Nan stared, hearing the melody played by its contrasts—the leaves and the lumber, the sky and the ground.

Enchanted, she gazed from one print to the other, marveling at the wholly different aspects two such similar structures presented. If there had ever been cause to worry that a show consisting entirely of churches might be boring, there was no cause for worry now.

"These are fantastic, Spence! Rem will be out of his mind." She scanned them again with growing wonder. "The texture, the focus—"

She heard the pride in his mild response.
"They'll do." Then he paused, his glance returning to the envelope. "Tell me what you think of
the others."

Anticipating different views of the same two
churches, she spilled the remaining photographs
out on the desk.

Then she drew back in astonished delight that
broke over her like sun rays. It was her own face
leaping up from the desk. Instead of additional
views of the churches, the prints were of her—
the photos Spence had shot on the beach.

At her back Spence murmured, "Do you see
how beautiful you are?"

Everything she had wanted him to say on that
upsetting day, his photographs said now. There
were twelve prints in all, each one stunningly
adoring of every feminine charm she possessed.
More than that, each was a study of human
traits—stubbornness, vitality, anger, arro-
gance.... As quickly as a magician, Spence had
captured a dozen moods. Click—and the in-
tangible was on film. Once more he had proved
that in his hands the camera was a powerful instrument of subtle articulation. The work of
many artists had impressed her, but Spence's
skill was overwhelming.

Turning to him, she was unaware that he
could read on the face he knew so well everything she was feeling.

"Oh, Spence. What can I say?"

His voice caressed her hoarsely. "I think you've said it."

"I can't stop looking at them." Her own trained eye had already deftly separated the image she met each morning in the mirror from the faces looking back at her. As Spence had photographed her, she was much more than a woman he found beautiful and desirable. She was any woman, *all* women, bound up in a fierce, momentary battle with air and water and human emotions.

Humbly she said, "These belong in a show of their own."

He put his hands on her shoulders and turned her around. "Yes, and they'll have it someday. But for now I've only begun to photograph Nan Blake." His husky voice moved over her, as warm and intimate as a touch. "If I looked the world over I'd never find a subject more intriguing or more endlessly fascinating."

Her breath caught in her throat. "That's the ultimate compliment, isn't it?" The full meaning of the gift he had given her was just beginning to dawn on her, and her voice trailed off in a whisper of wonder. "What more could a woman want?"

"She'd better want more of me." His arms came around her with a sudden fierceness. "Yesterday was hell without you."

A surge of joy drove everything else from her mind. "It was hell for me, too." Yielding to his embrace, she buried her face in his shoulder. At once the rough cloth of his coat cutting into her cheek recalled his suit-hunting expedition to Summerside—and whom he had asked to go with him. "Spence—" Her heart froze inside her. "What about Cate?"

He murmured between the kisses he was dropping along her brow, "What about Cate?"

"Josey says . . . ." The words stung her tongue. "Josey says you're going to marry Cate."

She heard his low chuckle. "Dear matchmaking Josey. And of course you believed her."

"Of course I did." But already she was breathing easier. "Who would know better than your sister?"

"I would. Cate would. And she and I have never discussed marriage."

"You've taken her out."

"Dozens of times." Spence drew back to look at her. "We've passed some pleasant evenings while you were holed up here stewing in your negative juices." His tone softened. "Cate is a good companion," he added gently. "She's a fine woman. I hope we'll always be friends."

Life tingled back through Nan's veins. "But you aren't in love with her?"

He raised his right hand and intoned solemnly, "I never have been, I never will be. My darling Nan," he scolded lightly, "I'm in love with you."

The blunt declaration took her breath away. "You've never said so."

He reached around and dangled the prints in front of her. "I've said so twelve times—twelve times oftener than you have."

Then suddenly he was grave again, gripping her shoulder, pinning her with his gaze. "I can't claim your experience with love, Nan. I don't know what the boundaries are or how far love reaches or how long it lasts. I don't know whether we can spend a week together or a month or a lifetime. But until we're sure, if you leave me I'll come after you. I don't care how far you run or how long it takes, I'll bring you back."

The love she had kept in check for so many weeks burst through the bonds she had imposed upon it. "You know how crazy this is, don't you?" She took his face between her hands, reveling in its weathered roughness and the angular strength that gave strength to her. "We're odd pieces cut from different cloth. We'll make a terrible mess of both our lives."

"You don't believe that, not with your heart."

"I do believe it." Her eyes filled suddenly. "But somehow, somewhere, I fell in love with you, anyway."

IN NAN'S ROOM Spence laid her down to undress her, moving with a swift, delicate tenderness that was heightened by his eagerness to make her his.

But Nan's eagerness matched his. The floodgates of her passion were open at last and every delay seemed an eternity.

When he was finally out of his own clothes and at her side, her excitement unfurled in a profusion of kisses, in a flurry of touches, mutual and sustained and tormenting beyond anything she had ever experienced.

Clasping her arms around his bare shoulders, she breathed into the thick hair that curled on his chest. "I hear your heart."

He breathed harshly against her neck. "It's stampeding."

"Like mine."

Hungrily he sought her lips, his mouth following the outline his fingertips circumscribed before it. He drank deeply of the love she offered like nectar and then moved on to taste the white curve of her throat, to kiss the fragrant valley between her breasts and the firmly rising swells that led to her standing nipples.

"How beautiful you are," he moaned. "My lovely elusive Nan."

"Not 'elusive'." She saw again the vivid, soul-searching photographs he had made on the beach. "No one knows me as you do." A fresh surge of yearning let him know her even more intimately. The palms of her hands flattened and slid down over his hardened thighs. "Tell me again, Spence, that you love me."

His heated voice shook with desire. "You aren't listening." He brought her astride his narrow hips and turned wonder-filled eyes upon her perfection. "With every breath I'm telling you—with every touch." He pulled back the curtain of hair that swept down across his face as she leaned to kiss him. "I love this mouth...I love these eyes." His thickened voice spread over her like honey. "I love this button nose and this little pink ear—"

Suddenly they couldn't wait any longer for fulfillment. Except for the brief moment of shifting that brought them together there was no reason to wait...no clothing to hamper the powerful thrust of his entry...none to hold back her joyous arching to receive him. No interfering voices came out of the past; no guilt intruded. There was no dread, no doubt. There was only a shining instant of perfect union, a pinpoint of exquisite sensation that exploded all at once into a tangible force that flooded their bodies.

"Nan—" Spence moaned. "Oh, my darling—"

Nan echoed his endearment and entered an ecstasy she had never dreamt was possible.

Their love peaked in a rapturous rush, and then a long, slow period of adoring caresses began. Spence's touch, as in his art, was sensitive and knowing, artfully drawing out every exquisite response of which she was capable. With expert tenderness he searched out the soft, forbidden pleasure spots of her body and quickened them with deft, caring strokes that struck fire from ashes and triggered new responses of his own.

Finally they lay back against the pillows, contemplating with languid exhaustion their fading pulsations, soaking up contentment from limbs that were still entwined and whispers that passed sleepily between them, while the sun rose in the sky and the rest of the world went about its mundane business.

10

SPENCE AND NAN dozed and then they woke again and kissed. Spence propped himself up on an elbow and treated himself to a long, languorous look at the treasure beside him.

"Nan," he said huskily, "do you have any idea how beautifully made you are?"

Her gaze caressed the muscled line of his torso. "*You're* beautifully made."

"You're too wonderful to believe."

"All these compliments—" She made a soft, scolding sound with her tongue. "I'll grow sleek as a cat. I won't want to do anything but lie on a silk pillow and be petted."

He bent his head and kissed her creamy shoulder. "Sign me up to be first in line."

She ran her fingers through the springy black hair falling over his temple. "There won't be any line—only you, only me." Then her look of contentment dimmed. "What if I'd never come here?"

"That could never have happened." He brought his blue eyes to rest on her lips. "I was waiting. I've told you before, what happened to-day was foreordained, a branding."

"A long time ago I was branded."

He was amused. "When? Where?"

"In your studio." Her shyness surfaced in the ducking of her head. "The first time you kissed me."

He lifted her chin and made her look at him. "You never let on."

"I did. I told you in dozens of ways how much I care for you. I stayed on here when we both knew I ought to go. Remington Ware's right-hand lady carried your camera cases and tagged along behind you like a puppy. I never would have cried about Davey in front of anyone but you."

Spence bopped her lightly on the nose. "There's that name again."

"What's in a name?" Nan teased, relaxed again but unable to stop the wistful note that crept into her voice. "I won't talk about Davey if you won't mention Cate. Thinking of Cate makes me sad, and I'm too happy to be sad."

He slid an arm beneath her shoulder and drew her close. "Why should Cate produce that kind of effect?"

"You promised not to talk about her."

"I didn't promise. Why, Nan?"

"Looking at her that day in the café, I could see how much she loves you." Nan's gaze clouded. "I haven't forgotten how it hurts to love and not be loved in return."

"Cate's wounds have all healed," Spence comforted her. "She knows that love can't be forced or made to fit a mold or offered to someone just to keep from hurting her feelings."

"But she must have had new hope lately."

Spence gave her a bemused look. "Why do you say that?"

"You've been going out. You took her to Summerside."

"She was there when I was ready to leave, and it was obvious she expected to go along."

Nan was quiet, rearranging her impressions. "Did Josey set it up?"

"I'm sure she did. For my own good, of course," he added, smiling wryly. "I imagine Cate thought the invitation came from me."

Nan sat up and pulled her knees to her chin. A few shimmering strands of hair fell down across her breasts.

Reverently Spence gathered them up and tucked them behind the pink ear that fascinated him. "Now what?" he said when he saw the thoughtful look she turned on him.

"Did Josey tell you about our quarrel?"

"Not the details, thank heaven."

"We were quarreling about you."

His index finger moved down her spine with a lingering stealth, stopping where her hips began. "Did you know there's a dimple here?"

"There are two. Are you listening?"

"Two," he confirmed with a nod of satisfaction, and leaned around her to plant a kiss on each one. "Yes, I'm listening. You and Josey got in a spat over me."

"She won't marry Beau because you're not married."

"Hopeless idiocy."

"I told her that. It made her angry."

Spence chuckled. "Can you blame her? Would *you* like to be called an 'idiot'?"

"I was more tactful than that." Nan bit her lip. "Well, slightly more tactful. I won't say I wasn't frank. It's so absurd of her to keep putting off Beau just because she thinks you're so helpless you can't look after yourself."

"Not to discount Josey's love," Spence said mildly, "she's more afraid I won't look after the house . . . left to my own devices I might burn the place down when I'm making baloney sandwiches or boiling potatoes. She can't stand the thought of my socks in the parlor and unmade beds and clutter in her kitchen."

"Maybe you should move out, then. You want her to have the house, anyway."

Spence chuckled. "Logic and precision. May I move in with you?"

"Be serious."

He drew her to him. "I am serious, my darling."

"We're talking about Josey now."

"And me, out in the snow and the wind." He

tickled her lightly in the ribs. "Wouldn't it make you feel terrible to know I was out in the cold, homeless and starving somewhere all because of you?"

"I can see we're getting nowhere fast with this conversation."

"Nan, my darling." He shifted to get a better look at the soft flush on her cheeks and the satin sheen on her breasts. "It's no good interfering with other people's lives. Most of the time, no matter what they say to the contrary, they're doing exactly what they want to do. If they had a chance, they wouldn't change their circumstances a dot or a tittle."

"Are you saying that Josey doesn't want to marry Beau?"

"I'm saying that she's in no hurry to upset the nest she's in now. She's comfortable leading the familiar life she's always led. Why should she change it?"

Nan responded quickly. "So she could have her own home!"

Spence shrugged. "She already has a home, one she's loved all her life. She has a husband, too, for all practical purposes." In answer to Nan's troubled look he added, "Beau and Josey are mature adults who have cared for each other for a very long time. I think we'd be naive to assume that the wedding bed would hold many surprises."

"Don't you think Josey wants children?"

"I do, but they've become more like dreams than possibilities." An impish grin lifted the corners of his lips. "And when her maternal instincts act up, she has me to boss around."

Nan felt a rush of love for the way he always managed to lighten even the soberest subject, but she couldn't entirely agree. "That's all the more reason you ought to get out from under her wing."

"When it suits me, I'll move. But I won't be doing it to accommodate Josey unless she specifically asks me to. That wouldn't be fair to Beau, or to her."

"I don't follow your reasoning."

His gaze softened and he touched her cheek lightly. "It's simple, my love. Josey has to take the responsibility for her own decisions. If she marries Beau it has to be because above everything else she wants to be his wife. It mustn't be because Beau or I or you finally made it convenient enough for her to fit him into her nest."

Nan's brown eyes misted. "You're a very wise man, my darling."

He cocked an eyebrow. "The wisest thing I can think of now is for you to kiss me."

Nan leaned willingly into his embrace, but even as the rapture of his touch began to stir her blood again, she wondered how much of his wisdom Spence had carried over into his own life.

FOR A WEEK after Nan's surrender to Spence, she let the days slip by like pearls on a string, not counting them, just enjoying the beauty of each one, following heedlessly the easy, unhurried pace Spence set as if it were their honeymoon.

They lolled away one whole morning at the Micmac Reservation and then rode slowly through the countryside, stopping whenever Spence wanted to show her something—the cross-country ski trails or the paths the horse-drawn sleighs would later follow across the snow into the woods.

"Winter is a wonderful season here," Spence told her when they leaned side by side against a weathered old shed in a lovely patch of shadow and sun. "It's the season when islanders know best the magic one can find in a place apart. For a few weeks we're relatively isolated. The strait ices over, the ferry schedules are cut." He brought Nan under his arm to shelter her from the wind. "We snuggle into our houses and let the gales huff and puff."

"And then it's spring." Nan's eyes took on a faraway look. Josey had described to her the thrill of seeing the first daffodils poking up through the crusty earth and blue jays flashing through the bare trees. Nan felt now that she loved the island almost as much as Spence. The excitement of city life still called and she missed the stimulating interchange of ideas she was exposed to at the gallery, but the easy rhythm of the island had gotten into her bloodstream, and she was mesmerized by a happiness she had never known. Largely this was due to the love she shared with Spence, but she made no effort to separate and categorize her feelings as she had done once. Spence's life was intertwined with the island life, and because of him, so was hers. It was enough to know that.

She turned in his arms and touched his face. "Have I told you lately how much I love you?"

His softening gaze poured over her while the pure blue of his eyes memorized every feature of her flowerlike face. "Wasn't it a lifetime ago that you knocked on my door? Nothing that matters existed before then."

Their lips met. Lips that knew each other so well they had devised a language of their own—nibbling pressures like hide-and-seek were the signal for foreplay; greedy deepening kisses communicated their need to savor the nectar that spilled from their tongues. . .and a thundering up from their souls signaled the surging power of mouth against mouth, craving. . .demanding. . . .

Inside the shed there was the soft, musty sweetness of hay. They hastened to lie down upon it, taking up the warmth the sun had bestowed on the straw as they slipped out of their clothes and made love to the sounds of the soughing wind and the strong, steady throbs of their hearts beating in unison.

Another day they spent with Beau at the fox farm. Nan followed him around like a studious apprentice while Spence trailed after them, snapping photographs of Nan in front of sly, animal faces looking on from their cages.

It was heaven, Nan thought, each time Spence held her or adored her with his eyes. She lost track of time, measuring it now as nothing when Spence was with her and as eternity when he was away.

But on Tuesday morning when Spence came by the cottage to pick her up, a sense of professional responsibility had overtaken her again. An early-morning telephone call from Remington Ware had reminded her that there was an outside world moving full steam ahead. While Rem talked, she realized that she hadn't opened her schedule book in days and that the weekend ahead would be lost for work since Spence would be away attending his friend's wedding.

As soon as she and Spence were in the car he mentioned the wedding. "You're coming with Josey and me to Charlottetown, aren't you?"

"Spence, I don't think so," Nan began hesitantly.

"It's our most impressive city," he urged. "You ought to have a look at it."

"I want to. I will sometime. Maybe later in

the month if we have some free time, you and I
can ride over there."

"What's wrong with this weekend?" he persisted. "Sunday morning we could go to the
oldest Anglican church on the island. Afterward
we might stop by Providence House or the Art
Center if you prefer—"

What he was describing sounded wonderfully
unstructured, like more of what had made her
so happy for days. Looking at Spence, she imagined light and music surrounding them as she
tossed responsibility to the wind, doing what
she pleased and to heck with the workaday
world!

But the Nan Blake who had dutifully trudged
to the crest of Boston's art world poked her head
out with a nagging reminder. Remington Ware
was counting on her to pull things together here,
to shape up the kind of spectacular show that
Spence's work deserved. Reluctantly she said, "I
really can't spare the time for a weekend jaunt
right now."

To an artist dragging his heels in Boston she
would have added as tactfully as she could,
"*You* can't spare the time, either."

But Spence was different...special...one of
a kind, cast from an Olympian mold. He had his
own inner clock and she trusted it—or at least
she was trying very hard to. He would make up
for lost time later, she told herself. At the finish

line he would leave everyone else standing dead-still at the starting post.

"Anyway—" She smiled in an effort to ease her disappointment in not being able to go with him. "If I went to Charlottetown I'd spoil the trip for Josey, I'm afraid." Their misunderstanding still remained unsettled. The few times the three of them had been together since the quarrel Josey had ignored the obvious change in the relationship between Spence and Nan. They couldn't be near each other for five minutes without touching or drifting off into private little reveries that Nan believed would have pleased Josey if she wasn't convinced again that Cate was the right woman for Spence. The coolness between them made Nan ache to put things right.

Turning back to Spence, she made a suggestion. "How about dropping me off at the Question Mark while you're in town picking up your film? I can have a chat with Josey and you can stop for me on your way back."

"I picked up the film yesterday after I let you off." He steered the car onto a road that led in the opposite direction from the farm. "Anyway, Josey's busy cleaning house this morning. Trying to talk to her when she's dispatching dust is like chasing a newspaper in the wind. You'd be better off waiting for a calm day to propose a truce."

Nan sighed. "How will I know when it's a calm day?"

"I'll arrange a signal. Two winks by land, one if by sea."

"Thanks a million, Paul Revere." She stared out at the smooth brown fields. "I wish I could see her today."

"Today, my dear, we have other fish to fry." Spence turned up the heater and adjusted a vent so that a warm flow of air cut the chill in the car. "There's a church I want to shoot near Kelvin Grove, and then we're going on to Cavendish Beach for a picnic."

Nan tried to think of a way to tell Spence gently that their lovely, leisurely days were over. "Isn't it too cold for a picnic?"

"We'll build a fire," he returned confidently. "This time of year the beach is at its best. For one thing, the sand is finally visible instead of three thousand bikinis and four or five acres of sunburned torsos."

Nan mused on how pleasant it would be watching the waves roll in, smelling the wood smoke. But taking time for a picnic and allowing a couple of hours for the inevitable lapses that loving each other demanded meant the sun would set before they accomplished a thing.

She reached for her red notebook. "I don't think I have a listing for a church near Kelvin Grove."

"That doesn't mean there isn't one there."

Spence's airy response caused a nervous flutter inside her stomach. After Remington Ware's call she had rechecked the work that remained to be done if they were to have enough prints for the show. They were running five days behind the projected schedule she had set up when Spence signed his agreement with Rem. She made a few scribbles in the margin of her notebook. Adding two more days for the lost weekend, they'd have to make up ten days work.

Nervously she said, "I love to look at those gray-and-white sea gulls, don't you? Look how they step over the furrows, as if they owned the island."

Spence pulled her against his side. "Who wants to look at sea gulls when *you're* here to look at?"

She leaned up to kiss his cheek. "You're spoiling me, you know that."

"Will you be beastly when I'm finished?" His blue eyes glittered, holding her glance. "Will you be naughty and disgustingly unapproachable?"

Nan snuggled closer. If he wasn't worrying, why should she. "Only to bill collectors and cute teenage girls selling magazine subscriptions." But she couldn't resist taking a peek at his watch. "What time is it, Spence?"

Her own watch was tucked away in her purse,

a concession she had made when Spence threatened to throw it in the sea unless she stopped checking every movement of the hands.

"It's not time for lunch," he said, "and it's too late for breakfast. Any more questions?"

She couldn't help herself. "Yes—one. The church at Kelvin Grove. If we keep adding churches to our files, how are we going to make our deadline?"

"If we get in a squeeze," he said comfortably, "we can always drop one or two of the others."

"Is it a good idea to switch around what we've already settled on?"

"What isn't a good idea," he said in a sterner tone, "is locking ourselves so rigidly into a schedule that we can't take the morning off if we want to."

"You'll be taking two mornings off at the end of the week—and two afternoons."

His head swung around. "Who's keeping score all of a sudden?"

"I am." Nan's cheeks burned, but her professional reflexes enabled her to keep her tone light. "That's my job."

"Oh, I see." Spence matched her tone, but an unfamiliar edge sharpened his. "Well, my job is to put feeling into my work." He turned his attention back to the narrow road they were following. "What I feel like this morning is shooting two rolls of film in Kelvin Grove." He gave her another look. "Or three if the spirit moves me."

Nan kept a tight rein on the turmoil inside her breast. Part of her was in hearty agreement with him. A man of Spence's talents worked best with no restraints. She knew that. But in this case they were so short of time...so dangerously near the edge of disaster....

Still, she was able to say calmly, "Okay, fine. Shoot whatever you want to. We'll just have to remember that we'll be working twice as hard later to catch up."

"Not necessarily. We'll see when the time comes."

All at once her control snapped. "I can already see. Out of three rolls of film, you may get one print you'll consider good enough to use. We need *three* good prints this morning and that many this afternoon if we want to keep our heads above water."

Spence pulled off abruptly onto the side of the road and turned around to face her. "To quote an old Southern gentleman, 'Frankly, my dear, I don't give a damn.' We can sink to the muddy bottom or not, it's all the same to me. I made it clear when you got me into this that I wouldn't allow you to pressure me."

Nan's blood thumped against her eardrums. "Of your own free will you signed a contract with the gallery. Don't you intend to honor it?"

"The contract I signed had an *if* clause, remember? If I can't make the deadline for the January show, I'm excused until a later date."

Nan's throat closed so tightly she could hardly force her words out. "The understanding was that you would conscientiously try!" The day after she had seen the Tignish church print and the one made in the maple grove she had privately assured Rem that there were no problems, that everything was moving ahead as planned. And now Spence was quoting the fine print, as he had every right to do, except that unknowingly he was smashing her career to bits.

He saw the pain in her eyes and suddenly his expression changed. "Hey, wait a minute." Tilting her chin up, he probed gently with his searching gaze. "This isn't like you. What's the matter? Did you get up on the wrong side of the bed?"

The swift change in his mood melted her. "I'm sorry, Spence. I'm acting like a shrew, I know."

"Acting," he murmured against her hair. "That's the key word. You couldn't be shrewish if you tried."

Cradling her shoulders, he nestled her protectively against his chest. His lips moving along her brow dropped kisses gentle and provocative. "I know what's upset you," he whispered. "You haven't been properly loved this morning, Miss Blake."

"I feel so uneasy, Spence. The weeks are slipping by so fast—"

"We'll deal with that later." He brought his lips to hers. The fires he could light with only a look blazed up in an ardor she could barely suppress.

"Someone will see us, Spence—"

But with his lips closing over hers, prying eyes couldn't matter. Nothing mattered except the tingling joy his touch brought. What was a wasted morning, a missed deadline? In his arms she was the most cherished being in the universe.

11

WHEN NAN OPENED HER EYES again, Spence was gazing down at her with the look that was always a prelude to lovemaking. Unbidden, her sense of responsibility reasserted itself. "Spence, we'd better be on our way."

"What if we scrap the whole day and go back to the cottage?" he said hoarsely.

"Darling, I'd love that but—"

"Half the day?"

"What about the church in Kelvin Grove?"

"We can shoot it tomorrow." But he saw her look of dismay and sat up, sighing. "All right, slave driver, I get the message." He reached for the key in the ignition. "Open your little red book and point me in the right direction."

Loving him more each moment, she put a restraining hand on his sleeve, ready to change her earlier plans. "Do what you want to. Whatever you decide is fine with me."

He laughed softly. "I believe I've corrupted you, Miss Blake. Are you really willing to stop straightening the shoes in your mother's closet and live a little?"

His teasing tone cut her and the hurt showed in her eyes. Quickly he took her in his arms again and said with his mouth against her hair, "Forgive me, darling. I forget sometimes what a serious business life is for you."

"It isn't," she denied. "But I don't know why it's so wrong to make a few plans and try to stick by them."

"It isn't wrong," he murmured. "It's just such a waste."

"A waste of what?"

"Of the spontaneous pleasures a day can hold if you just let it happen."

Nan moaned. "For you, maybe. But for us ordinary mortals, nothing gets accomplished when a person lives like that."

Spence was quiet for a moment, holding her. Then he released her and started the car. "You're shivering. I guess it is too late in the year for a picnic. We'll ride over to Rosehill, instead. That's one of your listings, isn't it? And then we'll have lunch in St. Eleanor's and see about the church in that area and the one over toward Travellers Rest."

Nan's chin trembled. "I've spoiled your day, haven't I?"

"No, sweetheart. You're right. We need to get on with our business like two sensible adults and stop fooling around." He turned a crooked smile on her. "But I warn you, my dear. I may finish the whole damned collection in a week, and if I do—" He gave her a lecherous look and brought his voice down to a growl. "If I do, you'd better watch your step, sweetheart."

SPENCE WAS AN ANGEL for the rest of the week, sticking without complaint to the rigorous schedule Nan mapped out for him.

On Saturday morning when she waved him off to Charlottetown with Josey in the front seat beside him, she felt only a twinge of regret that she wasn't going along. She would miss him. She was missing him already and she knew the feeling would intensify when night closed in and the empty cottage grew to twice its size. She read into Spence's subdued wave of farewell the same reaction. But it was gratifying to see Josey smile again, and maybe a whole weekend in the company of her brother would further sweeten her mood.

Besides, Nan thought, climbing into her parked car in front of the Question Mark, Spence had photographed so industriously since Tuesday, he had left her a mountain of work to sort through.

Backing out of the driveway, she headed toward O'Leary for the darkroom supplies Spence needed and for a few supplies of her own. She had a surprise planned. If matting board and tacks were available in O'Leary, she intended to mount the church prints that had collected so far on her cottage walls. When Spence returned on Sunday night it would be to a minigallery opening all their own. Somewhere in O'Leary she hoped to find a bottle of champagne, too, and if caviar was out of the question, at least she could substitute salmon pâté to round out the celebration.

Driving along, she thought with satisfaction of how much Spence could accomplish once he set his mind to getting his work done. The routine she had devised was demanding, there was no denying that. But by getting up at daybreak and getting on the road as soon as the sun was high enough to clear the air, they had added two churches a day to an already-full schedule.

On Thursday Spence had shot seven churches—a record number Nan hadn't been sure he could manage. He had printed up the week's work the evening before and handed it to her without comment as he and Josey were leaving. From the thickness of the envelope it was apparent that a majority of the shots had won his approval.

All the way to O'Leary she toyed with the idea of pulling off the road and taking a look at the contents of the envelope. Spence's finished photographs always gave her a tremendous thrill. There didn't seem to be any point in torturing herself by waiting to look at them until she got back to the cottage.

She did wait, however, until she pulled into a

parking space on O'Leary's main street, and then with a tingle of anticipation she took the prints out and spread them on the seat beside her.

Her first reaction was a queer sensation in the pit of her stomach, then a dry mouth followed by a pounding heart. The photographs were good, very good. But they weren't excellent. Something indefinable was missing and though her practiced eye examined them minutely, it was impossible to say what. She stared at each one, trying hard to decide. The focus? It was perfect. The composition was perfect. If any other artist of her acquaintance beside Spence had made the photographs she would have endorsed them without a quibble. But she was so accustomed to the fire and splendor in Spence's work that the prints she was examining seemed flat and lifeless, more like pretty pictures off a calendar than works of art. None of them, with the possible exception of the two he had taken early on Tuesday, came close to meeting the standard Spence normally set for himself.

She thought numbly that if she had pushed him too hard he would have balked, so it couldn't be that. It couldn't be that his powers of perception had diminished, so it must be.... She licked her lips. Yes. Spence had spoiled her, she decided in a damp sweat of relief. If these were the pictures he had shown her the first day

she viewed his work she wouldn't have been disappointed. But instead she had seen extraor-
dinary samples of what he could do. All artists
had their peaks and their valleys. It was un-
realistic to assume that Spence, as special as he
was, could peak continually.

She looked at the pictures again, doggedly re-
fraining from comparing them with his previous
work. No one else had Spence's eye for detail.
The way he worked with shadows was uncanny.
There was nothing the matter with the prints.
The hectic week just past had jaded her. It had
taken the edge off her appreciation and made her
too critical. Spence was the most exacting judge
of his work. If he had found the slightest fault, he
would have torn up the prints in his studio.

Reassured, she pushed them carefully back
into the envelope. She took another minute to
compose herself, and then she set out with a
lighter heart to buy the darkroom supplies.
In the shop where she found them, mounting
board and tacks were available, too, but when
she paused at the counter to make her purchase
she found she no longer had any enthusiasm for
the preview showing. A sick feeling came over
her when she thought of tacking up the new
prints next to the old ones, and she turned away
with a wan smile at the clerk and walked out of
the shop.

She skipped her purchase of champagne and

pâté, as well, and was climbing back into the car to head home to her cottage when a woman's voice hailed her.

"Nan? Nan Blake! Hello!"

Nan's heart stopped. Cate Donohue was smiling at her from the sidewalk. Apprehensively she watched the other woman approach the car. "How nice to see you again, Cate."

Then suddenly she realized that her greeting was sincere. Cate was a strikingly beautiful woman, and her smile when she came alongside the car was as friendly and open as it had been the day Spence had introduced the two of them in the café in Miscouche. Nan's discovery about the prints had rocked her stability, and Cate's quietly confident countenance somehow restored the balance.

Leaning in the window, Cate said, "It's a gorgeous morning, isn't it? Are you and Spence out taking pictures?"

Nan shook her head regretfully. "Spence and Josey have gone to Charlottetown for the wedding. I've been shopping."

"I forgot about the wedding. Then you're on your own for the day. Can you come and have lunch with me?"

Nan found herself wanting to with all her heart. She dreaded looking at the prints again and going through the agony of trying to decide if the quality was really as far below par as she was again believing. But if the truth had to be faced it was cowardly to put it off.

She shook her head again. "I'd love to have lunch with you, Cate, but I've mountains of work to do."

Cate was unperturbed. "I'm sure you're busy, but you have to eat somewhere. I have everything ready. I just drove in to town to mail a letter. I'm going straight home this minute. You can follow me in your car."

"I really shouldn't. . . ."

Cate capitalized on her hesitation. "You really should," she told her firmly. "I promise to let you go by one o'clock at least. You'll have the whole afternoon for getting on with your business."

"Spontaneous pleasure," Nan was reminded, recalling Spence's words. If she ever needed the lift spontaneity could give, she needed it now. "If you're sure I won't be any trouble—"

"You'll be a joy," Cate assured her. "I've been hoping we could get better acquainted." She lifted her hand in a wave. "I'm in that green Chevrolet down the block. Just follow along."

Driving down the bumpy lane that led to Cate's house on the outskirts of O'Leary, Nan wondered what they would say to each other. What did they have in common besides Spence?

But she needn't have worried. Cate's charming house delighted her, and Cate had a wealth of stories to tell about each interesting item she had collected. While they spooned up clam chowder and nibbled the sandwiches Cate set in the middle of her kitchen table, they talked about the china from which they were eating.

"It's Dresden," Cate told Nan with a modest glow of pride. "Don't you love all the little flowers? It's a set that's been in the family for three generations. I'm sorry to say there are only these few pieces left."

Nan admired the cup she was setting down. "I'd be afraid to use them."

"Perhaps I should be, too," Cate agreed. "But do you know what my thinking is? I never expect to be married, so who should I save it for? Who's going to care when I'm dead and gone that there isn't a piece left for the antique hunters?"

"Oh, Cate—" A crushing weight filled Nan's chest. "You can't possibly know that your future is that settled."

"Oh, but I do." Cate's voice softened along with her expression. "I've only met one man I'd have and that's Spencer Gallant." She finished with a smile. "But he won't have me, so that settles that."

She saw the stunned look on Nan's face and went on quickly. "Do I sound self-pitying? I don't mean to." She put out her hand and rested it for a moment on Nan's. "And I don't mean to make you uncomfortable, either—though of course I've heard how famously you and Spence are hitting it off." Her eyes twinkled. "News gets around rather quickly on P.E.I."

Nan thought of the day she and Spence had kissed at the side of the road, and she wanted to crawl under the table.

But Cate went on, warmly reassuring. "I think it's grand that you and Spence are enjoying each other. I hope your relationship blooms into something lovely and lasting, and I wouldn't be at all surprised if it did. You're attuned to each other. The first time we met I could see that right away."

Nan murmured awkwardly, "I'm sure you and Spence have interests in common, too."

Cate agreed. "It's true that we've had lots of good times together. For a while I thought they might add up to something, but I gave up hoping that a long time ago." She raised her frank gaze to meet Nan's questioning look. "Spence and I are friends and that's all."

Spence's words exactly. Nan's heart lifted. "That's a disappointment to Josey, I'm sure."

"Ah, poor Josey." Cate laughed and shook her head. "She would so dearly love to marry off Spence. The unfortunate thing is that she's as blank as I am about what Spence is truly like."

Nan's heartbeat quickened. "Why do you say that?"

"Because she and I know him only superficially, though Josey would never admit it even if she realized it. Still, I'm as helpless as she is in doing anything about it."

Cate reached for the coffeepot and filled their cups again. "Spence and I are close in many ways, but we're poles apart in what concerns him most—his work."

Nan's tongue felt thick and heavy in her mouth as she thought of the prints in the car. "Why is that?"

Cate shrugged her shoulders and smiled sadly. "I'm like Josey. We have an eye for china patterns and cut glass and authentic antique rockers, but when it comes to understanding the quality of Spence's photographs, all we see are pretty pictures."

She moved her cup in a slow circle around the edge of the saucer. "He's very sweet and very polite whenever I comment on his work, but it's always clear that there's a wall between us that I'll never see over or penetrate. I realized some time ago that I'd never be any closer to him than I am right now." She fixed her gaze on Nan again. "I don't know the whole man and I never will."

Relief mixed with Nan's sadness as sorrow for Cate welled in her heart. "Maybe you know him better than you think."

Cate shook her head. "I don't mind telling

you that if I did, I'd give you a run for your money, Nan." She smiled faintly. "I love Spence, make no mistake about that. But I know my limitations. I could never make him happy even if he gave me the chance to try."

"I know that he cares for you a great deal." Nan swallowed. "He cares so much that at times I've been jealous."

Cate faced her directly. "Are you planning to marry him?"

Color flooded Nan's face. It was a question she had pushed as far back in her mind as she could. Hearing it spring suddenly from Cate's lips made her flounder for an answer. "I don't think I can discuss that right now."

"No, of course not. I shouldn't have asked." Cate got up and busied herself clearing the table. "Friends don't have any right to be so nosy."

"Cate, I'm sorry."

"You needn't be, Nan." She paused with her hands full of the pretty flowered china. "You're not responsible for my happiness or for Josey's, either, you know."

"You sound like Spence."

"I think like Spence." Cate sighed. "Except that I lack his sensitivities." She turned to look at Nan. "But you have them. You've known him only a few weeks but already he's shared a side of himself with you that I could never hope to know. You speak his language. You could make each other very happy."

Nan ached inside. There was so much Cate didn't know, so much she didn't know herself. "You're a good sport, Cate."

"Not because I want to be." Cate smiled wryly. "I'd rather stamp my foot and scream at Fate. I would if I thought it would do any good."

"I wish you weren't so fatalistic about meeting an agreeable man. P.E.I. is a small island, you know—"

Cate finished for her. "And out in the big wide world there are millions of men I haven't met. But I'm an island woman, Nan. This is where I belong and this is where I'm going to stay."

Nan was silent, thinking of how content with island life Spence was. A chill ran up her spine. That common thread might eventually draw them together again. Spence might never love Cate in the searing, tumultuous way that he and Nan adored each other, but it was possible that he might find Cate's steadiness more to his liking in the long run. As long as Cate was willing to let him follow his own course it might not matter that she had so little understanding of what the course was about.

Standing beside the table, Cate observed her pensive look. "Do you wish I hadn't stopped you in town this morning?"

For a fleeting instant Nan did wish that. But

gazing at Cate's open, intelligent face, she was glad they had been able to speak honestly with each other.

She said from her heart, "I'm glad you stopped me, and I wish you well, Cate—whatever happens."

12

IT WAS ALMOST ELEVEN on Sunday night before the headlights from Spence's car finally shone through the windows of Nan's cottage.

Coming wide awake from a nap on the couch, she told herself it was fortunate she had scrapped the plan for a surprise celebration. Neither of them would have appreciated it at this hour, even if it had been called for. Besides, she thought as she rushed to let Spence in, all she wanted now was to be in his arms.

He brought the cold in with him. His face was cold; his coat gave off the chill of winter. But his embrace was warm and enveloping and worth all the unnerving hours she had spent waiting for him.

"Nan, Nan—" He covered her face with eager kisses and held her close to his powerful body.

She clung to him, smoothing her hands over his shoulders, over the rough tweed of his coat sleeves. "It took you forever," she told him huskily. "Where have you been?"

He sat on the couch and pulled her down on his knees. "I got up early this morning and went over into King's County."

She nuzzled his face. "Where the strawberries come from?"

"Yes, that's right. It was a long ride back."

"Why did you go? Did Josey go?"

"Josey." He grimaced. "At the last minute Beau changed his mind about going to the wedding and came chasing after us. When he showed up in Charlottetown that was the last I saw of my dear sister."

"So you went off on your own." Nan felt a stab of annoyance at Josey—and at herself, too, for uselessly sacrificing precious hours she could have spent with Spence. "You had your camera along," she remembered. "Did you take any photographs?"

"A few. The woods are spectacular this time of year." He smoothed back her hair and kissed her lips again and the delicate skin beneath an earlobe, murmuring endearments as his mouth lingered over her flesh.

The familiar male scent of him filled Nan's nostrils like a heady wine. She closed her eyes, murmuring, "I'm sniffing you up."

"It's a mutual pursuit." He opened her blouse and brought his lips to her breast. When her rosy nipples were taut and glistening he laid her on the couch and turned his body to cover her.

He whispered thickly in her ear, "When did they start putting forty-eight hours in a day?"

"The morning you went away. Was it only yesterday?" She breathed into the warm hollow of his shoulder, where the scent of evergreen mingled with his own scent. For her the hours had seemed even longer while she battled with the knowledge that his latest work was inferior. When Spence was busy with his camera he lost all track of time, but alone in the cottage she had been aware of every empty minute ticking by.

She ran her hands up over his shoulders and down under the collar of his shirt. The warm, resilient flesh that seemed a part of her sprang up to meet her fingertips. She smelled his skin and his shaving lotion and his shirt, and the ache inside her deepened. She wanted to protect him from the bad news she had to tell him. She wanted to keep him safe from every blow life might ever inflict upon him.

Twisting in his arms, she brought her lips to his in a series of frantic little kisses that inflamed them both.

Spence said huskily, as if reading her mind, "Let's throw all the clocks away."

And the calendars, she wanted to add, but she whispered instead, "I have a better idea. Let's go to the bedroom."

Her eagerness touched him and fed his own

desire, but he took his time undressing her, making her wait while his hands and his lips praised the glowing column of her body, naked in the pale light from the bedside table.

"I need my camera now," he muttered with his mouth on the creamy curve of her shoulder.

"I don't need a camera to keep sharp my memories of you." She tantalized him with a subtle movement, bringing groans of desire from him. "I only have to shut my eyes," she murmured, "and you're there, against my eyelids."

A shudder of suppressed passion rocked him. "Against your eyelids is not where I want to be," he rasped out hoarsely. "Come to bed, you wanton witch."

But when he had her beneath him she was no witch, only a supple, adoring angel whom he caressed with such exquisite ardor that her craving peaked instantly and when at last he thrust into her they soared at once to ecstatic heights.

They passed another delicious hour making up for the endless time they had spent apart. When they were sated and had rested, they made a languorous game of dressing each other and then wandered back to the kitchen for coffee.

"We'll never sleep," Nan told him when he filled her cup the third time.

"I don't want to sleep." Spence still looked at

her as if she were more necessary than the air he breathed. "If I let you out of my sight again you might vanish like a bubble."

"I wish you could stay here tonight, but what would Josey think?"

"Whatever she likes." His fingers toyed with a wisp of Nan's hair. "Josey knows what's happening. Do you think she's blind?"

"I think she's choosing to be where we're concerned."

"This weekend may have mellowed her."

"Is there a chance of that?" Nan searched his face eagerly. "I've missed her friendship terribly."

"She's missed you, too." His gaze drifted over the shadowed planes of her face. "You could go over to see her tomorrow."

"Tomorrow evening, you mean." Nan thought nervously of the day ahead, of the conversation they would have to have and the reassessment of where Spence stood in regard to his work. "We're going to be busy until then."

"I have an idea." He paused, fidgeting with his coffee cup. "Why don't you sleep late in the morning and take the day off?"

"Not go with you?" Her heart leaped. Unknowingly he was offering her a reprieve. But she couldn't accept it. They needed every minute that was left to them, and even that might not be enough to pull the show together.

"Why shouldn't I go?" she said. "I've had the whole weekend off."

"You were supposed to have worked all weekend," he chided mildly. "Or did you loll around all the time I was gone?"

"The 'lollingest' thing I did was to have lunch with Cate." It seemed a hundred years ago that she had sat in Cate's quaint kitchen, spooning chowder from a flowered bowl.

"You had lunch with Cate?" Spence's pleased surprise showed in his lifted brows. "When?"

"Yesterday. I went over to O'Leary for supplies and ran into her in town."

"I've had the feeling you weren't fond of Cate."

Nan smoothed the dark hair on his arms and fought back the urge to enfold him against her breast. "That was before I knew that you loved me."

Spence was amused. "How does my loving you make Cate more likable?"

Her shyness showed in her muffled reply. "She isn't a threat anymore."

"She never was. I've never been in love with Cate, Nan."

"I know that. I mean, I really know it now. Cate knows it, too, so I don't have to be sad for her anymore." But Nan found it hard to go on. "She believes my understanding of your work makes you and me closer, that it rounds out our love in a way that would never be possible for her."

She went on talking for a minute, largely because she felt she owed it to Cate to represent her views fairly.

When she finished Spence made no comment, and Nan saw that while she was reviewing the lunch in O'Leary his mood had changed.

Trying to restore their closeness, she teased, "We talked for a long time about you."

"What was the general conclusion?"

"That you're enigmatic and mysterious. That you're the most gallant Gallant on the island."

"That covers a lot of territory."

She made her voice a resonant whisper. "You're a lot of man."

Spence gave her an absent smile. "So what about tomorrow? Shall I tell Josey you're coming over or not?"

Nan swallowed, confused now about everything and feeling isolated in her misery. "I won't have time for visiting."

"Oh, yes, I forgot that the calendar rules us." He fastened his gaze on her. "What's the quota for the coming week?"

"The same as for last week, I suppose." The moment she had dreaded was upon them. "Unless you object." She leveled her gaze on him. "If there's anything you want to say, Spence. . . ."

His expression softened suddenly, and he

leaned around the corner of the table and kissed her tenderly on the lips. "I'll say good-night. We're both tired. We'll need some sleep if we have another big day coming up."

Helplessly she watched him get up and pull on his coat. Wistfully she said, "I'm glad you're not afraid any longer that out of your sight I'll vanish like a bubble."

She wanted to lie down again in his arms and pretend that nothing had changed. That nothing ever would. But Spence had already moved toward the door. He paused with his hand on the knob and looked back at her.

"I love you, Nan. That's all that matters. That's all I want you to think about until tomorrow."

Her throat tightened. "Oh, darling, I love you, too." But deep inside she felt time crumbling beneath their feet. The work on the show had held them together. What if tomorrow even that crumbled?

13

WHEN NAN OPENED HER EYES the next morning sunlight was pouring into the cottage. The hands on her travel clock pointed to nine, and someone was knocking loudly on her front door.

In a flurry she sprang up, aware that she should have been dressed an hour ago and had breakfast ready and waiting for Spence.

But it wasn't Spence at the door.

Josey stood on the stoop, with a covered basket on her arm and an apprehensive smile quivering on her lips. "I woke you. I'm sorry."

"Thank goodness you did!" Nan stepped aside to welcome her in. "I should have been up hours ago." Shoving her hair back from her face, she glanced fearfully toward the yard. "Has Spence given up on me and gone ahead?"

The aroma of freshly baked bread filled the room as Josey set down her basket and lifted off the napkin. "He peeped in on you earlier to tell you he'd be tied up this morning, but you were still asleep, so I offered to come over later and let you know." She tried out her smile again. "Anyway, I had something to talk over with you."

Nan steered her toward the kitchen area, the realization seeping through her sleep befuddled brain that the house was warm. A rush of love filled her. Spence's doing. "Sit down," she told Josey. "I'll put on some coffee."

While she filled the pot and set it perking Josey kept silent, but when Nan turned around Josey burst out suddenly, "I've come to tell you, Nan Blake, that you've done me the biggest favor of my life."

Nan gave her a startled look. "What do you mean?"

"You shocked me into seeing what a fool I've been."

"Oh—" Nan sank into a chair, pushing to the back of her mind her thoughts of Spence. "I hurt your feelings, that's what I did. I said things to you that were none of my business."

"Like a true friend, Nan."

"I haven't felt like a friend. I've felt awful, and now you come bringing me this beautiful bread—"

"The bread is nothing." Josey waved her peace offering aside as if it didn't exist. "I should have fixed you a ten-course dinner. I will yet, any night you say."

Nan saw suddenly that what she had mistaken for a nervous humbling of pride was actually a state of elation. Josey's eyes were shining like stars and her cheeks were on fire with a wild kind of excitement that brought Nan out on the edge of her chair.

"What is it, Josey? What's happened?"

A rush of words spilled from Josey's lips. "Everything good, everything wonderful! And all because you had the good sense to take me to task in my kitchen that day. What you said to me boiled around in my brain for a week—oh, not because I was angry at you. Well, I was at first. Angry and humiliated. And then the truth began to dawn on me, and I got angry at myself and scared, because I thought it was too late to do anything about it. I was so ashamed. Then Saturday in Charlottetown, watching the bride come down the aisle with Beau sitting right next to me, not caring a hoot what his precious foxes were doing—"

She ran out of breath all at once. "The long and the short of it is, Beau and I are getting married!"

"Oh, *Josey!*" Nan flew around the table and met Josey halfway, laughing and reaching out to accept her hug.

"I wanted to come straight here last night and tell you," Josey babbled. "But Spence's car was out front and Beau and I still had so many things to say to each other—"

Nan couldn't stop her happy tears. "Why didn't Spence tell me?"

"He knew I'd kill him if he spoiled my surprise."

Relief flooded Nan as she realized all at once that Josey had given her the reason Spence had stayed away this morning. "Start at the beginning. I want to hear everything."

"You already know the beginning. The middle was just my adding up what you'd told me and balancing it out with common sense." Josey gave her another bear hug. "And the end is a wedding planned for a week from Saturday at the Question Mark!"

"Oh, Josey! I couldn't be more thrilled about you and Beau if I were getting married myself."

"Are you thrilled enough to stand up with me?"

Nan's lips parted. "Be in your wedding, do you mean? Oh, Josey, darling. I'd be honored! But won't Cate—I mean, you've been friends for such a long time—"

"I'm asking Cate to provide the music. But even if I didn't need her at the spinet, I'd want you as my maid-of-honor. There wouldn't be a wedding if it wasn't for you." Josey gave her a saucy grin. "I'll never be able to thank you enough for smacking me in the face with the truth."

"Love would have found a way to bring you and Beau together, Josey."

"Do you think so?" Josey's look turned starry.

"I feel romantic enough this morning to believe that's true. But just the same, I'm glad we didn't have to take the chance."

As soon as Josey left to rush over to the fox farm and say good-morning to Beau, Nan dressed and set out for the Question Mark. Halfway there she met Spence walking along the road toward the cottage.

Stopping her car alongside him, she saw that his camera was slung across his shoulder. He looked cheerful, as well, and her spirits lifted. As Josey was leaving she had passed on the warning that Spence was in a snit, up half the night stomping around in his studio. But looking at Spence, Nan decided that in Josey's eyes this morning, a snit meant any mood that wasn't as sky-high as hers.

Spence's greeting seemed to confirm that opinion when he leaned through the car window to kiss her lightly. "Well, if it isn't Miss Sleepyhead. So you're up at last."

Love spilled out of the smile she returned. Just the sound of his voice could set any day right. His hand on her arm pressed with gentle possessiveness into her flesh. Hope stirred, a hope that her uneasiness about his work had been only a bad dream scattered by the sunny morning and tossed like ashes into the wind. A new confidence told her that somehow they would sort things out. As she had said to Josey, love would find a way.

Returning Spence's light kiss, she murmured, "I'm sorry I missed you earlier. Thanks for warming the cabin, but I wish you had awakened me."

The skin around his eyes crinkled. "You looked too peaceful to disturb, all curled up like a little brown bear tucked in for the winter. So I took your picture, instead."

Her shyness surfaced. "Nothing too revealing, I hope." Then, tenderly gruff, she added, "Get in, or do you want to stand in the road all day?"

When he was settled beside her, he adjusted the lens on his camera and aimed it at her. She hardly noticed anymore when he took her picture. He had stopped showing her the prints long ago and she had stopped wondering what they were like. He must have a hundred shots of her by now, in all sorts of poses set against every kind of background—with straw in her hair, jam on her chin, dressed up, dressed down—but until this morning, always dressed. An erotic stirring along her spine made her look away from him as she started the car down the road.

"Where to?"

"Wherever you say." He snapped another picture, this time of her profile set against the brown field beyond the window. "You're the lady in charge."

Mentally she flipped through her red notebook. Most of the morning was gone, but there was still the afternoon. They could postpone talking about the last batch of prints until later this evening over a drink. Maybe if they worked very hard in the time that was left they could still catch up. "Shall we go to Kincora, then?"

"Kincora is fine." His moodiness of the evening before had vanished completely. "Anyplace is fine." He set his camera aside and faced her. "You haven't told me what you thought of Josey's news."

Nan's eyes lit with happiness. "I thought it was wonderful. It thrilled me to see how excited she was."

"She owes all that excitement to you."

"She seems to think so. I'm just glad she's happy and that we're friends again. What did you think of her news?"

"That it was high time," he said, "and past time." The fingers of one of his hands sifted through a blond swirl on her shoulder. "I haven't told Josey yet, but I'm legally renouncing all claim to the Question Mark. I'm moving out."

"Spence, that's very generous."

He gave her a wry smile. "You suggested it."

"It was your idea a long time before I said anything."

He grinned. "But I needed a bomb set off under me to carry through on it."

Nan tried not to think of how similar the re-mark was to Josey's comment that she had smacked her in the face with the truth. An unflat-tering picture of herself rose in her mind. Nan, the tyrant, busily cracking her whip. But at least her intentions were good, and for Josey and Beau, things had turned out well.

She said to Spence, "Where will you go when you move?"

"Maybe down to one of the beach cottages, if I can work out darkroom arrangements. Maybe I'll trade places with Beau and rent the fox farm."

Moistening her lips, she said, "Maybe after the show you'll decide to settle again in the States."

"That's possible." He squinted at a line of maple trees against the horizon. "I could go back to Harvard and get a business degree."

The idea was so ludicrous in the light of where his talents had carried him that Nan laughed in spite of her anxiety. "You're not worried any longer about stocks and bonds up to your arm-pits?"

"I don't know. Maybe I'd like making pots full of money, being rich." His look sharpened. "Would you?"

The directness of his question took her aback, but she was more unnerved by the seriousness she sensed underlying it. "Making money isn't something I've thought much about."

"I see." He paused. "I thought it might be a

yearning for riches that makes you so industrious."

"Of course not." It stunned her that such an idea could even have occurred to him. *Industrious*. That was hardly the way she pictured her dedication to her work. "I thought you knew me better than that."

"I've claimed to, haven't I?" His hand was on her nape, massaging it gently. "I do know all the colors of your moods," he mused, "and your vulnerabilities, your softness and your sinewy toughness. But I don't know your ambitions."

She recalled Davey's relentless ambition and how much she had hated what it did to him. "I'm not an ambitious person."

"Are you sure?" Spence said softly. "You've been very ambitious for me."

She felt hollow inside all at once—and cold, chilled clear through to the bone. "Could you roll up your window, please. There's a draft."

He closed the offending crack and then turned back to her, his blue eyes as clear as the strait on a summer day. "Have you examined the prints I gave you on Saturday?"

The bottom dropped out of her stomach. "Yes. Yes, I've examined them."

"Why haven't you commented?"

"I was waiting for you to say something."

"All right. I will. The January show is off. But

of course if you've examined the prints you already know that."

Blindly she steered the car off the road and shut off the engine. "Why didn't you tell me that last night?"

"It was too late for a heavy discussion," he said quietly.

Her heart cried out, *maybe it was too late the day I rang your doorbell.* "You're joking about calling off the show, aren't you?"

"I was never more serious in my life."

"But all your wonderful work—"

"It's wooden, Nan. Rotten."

Her voice rose with her panic. "I don't think you want a show! I don't think you care what happens to your career!"

Suddenly his hands locked round her wrists. "My career, no. My photographs, yes. You've never understood that the two are separate."

"I do understand! But they're separate only because you've chosen to make them so." She had the wrenching feeling that someone else was making this speech, someone she despised, while the real Nan Blake backed Spence one hundred percent. "Yes." She moderated her tone as she regained control of her emotions. "Yes, I endorse artistic freedom. But a successful career requires discipline, too, and your trouble has been that you'd rather coast along snapping pictures as you please."

"The kind of discipline you insist on produces nothing but trash."

The accusation cut through her to the quick. "Perhaps I *have* pushed too hard. If so, I apologize. The last thing in the world I wanted was to stifle your creativity. But I can't agree that the work you've done is trash. These last photographs don't represent your best work, but if they didn't have merit you wouldn't have printed them."

"I printed them," he said curtly, "because I didn't know a better way to show you that we've been wasting our time. Nan—" A new urgency took control of his voice. "I cannot work the way you want me to."

The chill that had begun in her bones spread through her bloodstream. Her reputation in Boston, all her successes seemed to crumble about her, inconsequential and stupid in the light of the colossal error she had made with Spence. She should have been the first one to stand back and let him work as he wanted to. Certainly she of all people recognized how necessary it was for an artist to have absolute freedom to create. Yet she had excused her eagerness to push him into the limelight because she loved him so much, because she wanted the world to see his marvelous photographs now, not five years from now.

All of the fire went out of her as the freezing

chill enveloped her. Slumping against the seat, she said, "You knew this when we started out a while ago. Why did you agree to go to Kincora?"

"At Kincora," he said in a gentler voice, "I'm going to do what I want to do." He slipped his arms around her and warmed her in his embrace. "If I have a feeling for the church there, I'll shoot it. If not, I won't. That's the way it has to be from now on. We're getting off the treadmill."

She let his words sink in slowly. Then in a small voice she said, "I'm glad, really." She managed a crooked smile that belied the tears that stood in her eyes. "Being the taskmaster isn't all it's cracked up to be."

Her effort to joke made him bend his head and drop a kiss on her lips. "Postponing the show isn't the end of the world, either. When we do get a show together we'll be glad we waited, and so will Remington Ware."

Nan sighed. "If he's speaking to us by then."

Spence frowned. "What do you mean?"

She swallowed hard. "The invitations for the January show were printed last week. The publicity has aired all over the Northeast."

"How can that be? I haven't given Ware the go-ahead for any definite arrangements."

"I have." Meeting his gaze, she trembled. "I gave it to him."

"My God, Nan!" He stared, incredulous. "The hell you did!"

She couldn't bear to look at him. "At the time I didn't see any reason not to. We were behind schedule, but I'd seen the Tignish-church print and the one taken in the maple grove. I was sure you could catch up."

"You spoke for me without even asking?"

She squeezed her eyes shut but still she saw his eyes like blue glaciers, his jaw set like granite. "It didn't occur to me that I was overstepping. Things were going so well—" Her voice cracked. "I know. What I did is inexcusable. If you can't forgive me, I won't blame you."

An eternity seemed to pass before he put his arms around her. "Oh, come on," he whispered finally. "It's not as bad as all that. We're in a mess, but we can get out of it. It's my fault, too. When you started stepping on my toes I should have thundered from Mount Olympus and made the earth shake." He tipped up her chin, trying to make her smile. "I played dead longer than I should have, and the mouse ran away with the cheese."

She gazed at him through the tears she was determined not to let fall. "You're talking as if all that concerns us is the Summerside Rotary Club Pancake Supper."

Spence laughed. "A year from now we won't even remember it."

"A year from now I'll still be looking for a job," Nan said glumly.

"Ware won't fire you."

"Of course he will. He should." She had never felt the power and comfort of Spence's presence as keenly as now. "He can't afford an assistant who schedules a show, then doesn't turn up with it."

Spence turned belligerently protective. "He can throw his damned invitations in the river and schedule someone else."

Nan patted the hand that lay tucked under her breast. "The kind of artists the Ware Gallery shows can't be recruited on ten minutes' notice. Rem can't call them up one morning and expect to hang their work in the afternoon."

"A while ago you accused me of not wanting a show," Spence chided. "I'm accusing you now of not wanting to work out this problem. Nan—" He took her face between his hands, his thumbs caressing the hollows of her cheeks with a tenderness that brought fresh tears to her eyes. "In all the hubbub we've forgotten the most important thing. We love each other. We can lick this thing together."

"I can't imagine why you'd even want to try. I've created such havoc. I wouldn't blame you if you stayed angry at me until the middle of the next century."

"We got in a yelling match," he murmured,

"but now it's time to be good to each other, to put monkey blood on our wounds and apply fresh Band-Aids."

She gazed at him in wonder. "No one I know gets into yelling matches and makes up. What's the matter with you?" Her tears began to fall. "Do you have a soft spot in your head?"

"I have a soft spot in my heart—for you." He took out a handkerchief and dabbed expertly at her eyes. "Now let's put Niagara Falls on hold and consider our options."

"All this has happened before," she said weakly. "Good Dr. Gallant administering his bedside manner."

"The thing to remember is that the patient recovered."

Taking the handkerchief, she blew her nose. When she was composed again she said, "Do we have any options?"

He didn't answer. He was busy taking her picture.

"Oh, Spence, for goodness' sakes!"

He tilted her chin deftly and clicked the camera twice more. "We have two. Number one is to call Remington Ware and explain."

Nan blanched. "I could never do that! What would I say?"

Spence shrugged. "You're good friends. Tell him you made a mistake. He isn't superhuman, is he? Surely he's messed up once or twice himself."

"What's option number two?"

A split second passed. "We make do with what we have and go ahead as planned."

Nan's eyes opened wide. "Do you mean go ahead on the twenty-first?"

"Yes."

"You'd really do that?"

"Not willingly. Not happily. But, yes—" he planted a kiss on the tip of her nose "—yes, I'd do it."

"Oh, Spence," Nan whispered, "I haven't any right to accept such a sacrifice."

He smoothed her hair back from her forehead and pulled her close against his chest. "It isn't a sacrifice if it's for you."

14

LOOKING PAST NAN into the mirror of a bridal shop in Summerside, Josey clasped her hands in a gesture of pure delight. "The search is over! That gown is perfect."

Nan agreed. The dress she saw reflected in the glass was simple but elegantly designed, a silky georgette the color of lilacs in early spring. Rows of narrow, flat ruffles angled gracefully from Nan's shoulder to her waist, where a wide sash of the same fabric flatteringly belted in the flaring skirt.

Josey herself had chosen a tissue-thin ivory silk, plain except for two exquisite lace inserts that formed a diamond at the base of her throat and then were repeated in the handkerchief hem that swept the floor.

The wedding was set for the following Saturday at two in the parlor of the Question Mark— renamed Fox Haven Farm by Beau and Josey the evening the four of them had celebrated Spence's generous gift. Spence would stand up with Beau as best man and the only guests would be Cate at the spinet playing the wedding music and a few close neighbors and friends.

The wedding day was Josey's birthday, as well. A caterer in Summerside had been put in charge of the small reception, but Cate had insisted on the privilege of baking the wedding cake herself.

On the way back to the farm after their shopping trip, Josey divulged further details.

"She's baking three layers—and icing it in white, of course. But she's dotting it all over with lilies-of-the-valley made of spun sugar." Josey glanced across at Nan with sparkling eyes. "That ought to look adorable, don't you think, especially with the birthday candles?"

Nan tried to picture it without showing her distress. "Candles on a wedding cake?"

Josey shook her head. "Not *on* it, around it. Haven't I told you? Cate has an antique birthday plate of pressed glass in the diamond-and-star pattern, which I think will be lovely, considering the design of my dress. All around the plate's rim are little holes for birthday candles. I counted once. Seventy-two. But thank heaven I won't require quite that many."

Nan laughed. "Will you make a wish before you blow them out?"

"A wish to end all wishes." Josey sighed. "Do you realize, Nan, that if I don't have a baby the first year, I'll be that much closer to being too old?"

Nan reached out to squeeze her hand. "Maybe you'll have twins. Who knows?"

Josey said fervently, "I can't think of anything nicer."

"You and Beau will make wonderful parents."

"We're talking as if I'm pregnant already."

Nan smiled fondly. "We'll give you a few more days." Then as Josey chattered on, her thoughts drifted back to her own problems. A few more days and she would be gone from P.E.I.

The wedding would take all of Saturday and then on Sunday Nan would board the ferry for Cape Tormentine in New Brunswick. By the start of the next week she would be back at work in the gallery, making the final preparations for Spence's show.

The closer the time came for her departure the worse she felt about the show. She and Spence had discussed it at length and oddly enough had traded their original views. Spence was the driving force now, encouraging Nan when her enthusiasm lagged. She dreaded the critics' reaction, but Spence expressed confidence they could pull it off if they hung the show in the manner of a retrospective, starting off at the head of the gallery with the inferior prints, giving the impression that they were earlier works.

"That's deceptive, you know," Nan told him glumly.

His answering look, quickly wiped away,

showed that he agreed, but he persisted in maintaining an optimistic front. "Nothing in the catalog will indicate that they are earlier efforts. The deception, if there is one, will be in the viewer's interpretation," he said. "There's nothing we can do about that."

"This is all my fault," she mourned.

"It's nobody's fault. It happened. We're taking care of it the best way we can."

"Oh, Spence, I'm not sure we are. You deserve so much better than this."

But Spence refused to listen to that kind of talk, and they spent the last hour before they said good-night not talking at all, but wrapped in a closer communion than they had ever shared before.

However, after Spence left, Nan found it impossible to sleep. In succeeding nights she fared no better, and when Josey let her out at the beach cottage after their shopping trip, her backlog of weariness suddenly took over.

Leaning back through the car window, she said, "Tell Spence I'm napping, will you, Josey? I think I may sleep straight through dinner."

Josey frowned. "Did I wear you out altogether in Summerside?"

"Heaven's no." Nan managed a convincing smile. "I loved every minute of it. I'm just sleepy all at once. Too many late nights catching up with me, I guess."

Josey's troubled look persisted. "I know what Spence is doing. He's trying to cram all the happiness he can into the few days before you leave. Do you have to go, Nan? Can't you just chuck everything in Boston and stay here forever?" She squinted hopefully. "It's not too late for a double wedding, you know."

"Josey, you're a darling." Emotion thickened Nan's voice. "But Spence and I aren't making those kinds of plans."

She didn't add that the subject of marriage had never come up. Once or twice she had felt Spence leaning in that direction, but as thrilled as she was she had steered the talk back to the crisis at hand. For Nan at least, coping with the gallery opening required all her energies. Nothing could be settled until the show was over, and when it was, there might be nothing left to settle except the dust of Spence's splendid career-that-might-have-been. He could easily have second thoughts about forgiving her, much less marrying her.

Waving Josey off, Nan went into the house, forlornly dragging her steps. The snug little cottage was still warm from her morning fire, but when she was undressed a clammy overlay of air sent her scurrying under the cozy comfort of Josey's flannel sheets.

Sleep. Nan longed for it and thought of Shakespeare's definition. If only it could "knit up the raveled sleeve of care." But just as it seemed she might drift off into oblivion she heard Spence's car turning into the dooryard. In a moment his key turned in the lock and then he was leaning over the bed brushing her lips with his.

"Didn't Josey give you my message?" She roused herself enough to twine her arms around his neck.

The breath from his murmured assent fell warmly on her throat. "I interpreted it as an invitation to join you."

She answered regretfully, "I'm really tired, darling. I can't lift a finger."

"No finger lifting required," he assured her, and peeled off his own clothes to stretch out beside her beneath the covers.

The warmth from his body flowed out to meet her, and she nestled against him, pressing her lips into the curly mass of dark hair on his chest. "Did you really come here to take a nap?"

"I came to hold you while you take one."

A familiar stirring began in her loins, but Spence was careful not to encourage it. Instead he settled her comfortably in the crook of his arm and with his other hand hypnotically stroked the hollow of her back until her breathing evened and she slipped off into slumber.

Nan woke at twilight to the faint calls of shorebirds winging in to the dunes. Shadows had filled up the room, changing the furniture into bulky gray lumps. Beside her in the bed Spence lay on his side, facing her. His eyes were closed and the even sound of his breathing might have lulled her back to sleep, except that she was too enthralled to close her eyes on the peaceful picture he made.

A silent prayer lifted from her soul. *Please, God*, she petitioned, *let him stay this untroubled always*.

But while she had slept her thoughts had cleared. A prayer, she mused as she went on watching Spence, required the supporting actions of the one who offered it. Instead of contributing to Spence's peace of mind, she had turned him away from the clear-sighted methods with which he had always approached his work. She had made him substitute schedules for intuitive timing, deadlines for the painstaking precision that made his best photographs the finest she had ever seen.

Right from the start he had warned her not to meddle with his technique, but she had been so sure she knew best.

She felt him stirring at her side and put her lips to his cheek to kiss him awake. His eyelids came up slowly, and when he saw her wistful look hovering over him, he smiled.

"I needed that smile," she murmured. "It's like a blessing."

Spence snuggled playfully against her. "Let me bless you with a few of my other attributes."

"That's a tempting offer," she returned softly, "but for the moment at least I have to turn it down."

"Why? Because it's half-past your dinner hour?" he teased.

Her heart began a painful thudding. "Because we have to talk."

"Let's make love, then eat, then talk."

"Please listen, Spence." She knew now what she had to do. Putting it off so many days was the cause of her exhaustion. If only Spence would agree. . . .

He caught the somber note in her voice and came up to a sitting position. "Okay," he said quietly. "Shoot."

"Do you promise not to say anything until I finish?"

"Cross my heart—but I won't hope to die." He kissed the pink curve of her ear. "I'm looking forward to a long and wonderful life."

"Oh, Spence—" her voice cracked with emotion "—I love you so much."

His own voice thickened. "If I could be allowed a few more succinct phrases before you begin—"

But she put her fingers to his lips. "Instead of phrases, hold me for a minute."

His strong arms wrapped around her. "I'll hold you all night if you want me to."

She forced her mind away from the tempting

haven he offered and sat up, pulling the flannel sheet over her breasts. "If I were a smoker," she told him shakily, "it might help to light up right now."

Concern showed in his voice. "You're really uptight about whatever this is."

She exhaled slowly. "I'm calling off the show, Spence." She heard his sharp intake of breath. "As soon as I get back to Boston I'm going to do as you said we should at first. I'll explain to Rem what happened."

Spence grabbed her shoulders. "Wait a minute!"

"He can get in touch with the media," she went on doggedly. "I expect a big mess, but the sooner it's cleared **up** the better. I'd leave tomorrow except for Josey's wedding."

"Will you be quiet and listen? The final decision on this subject has already been made. We thrashed it out days ago. The show is *on*. Do you understand that?"

She shook her head. "What I understand is the ruin I almost caused." She melted against him, burying her face in the hollow of his throat. "When I think that I could have spoiled the finest exhibition of photographs ever to be shown in Boston."

"Stop it!" Spence tightened his grip. "You're a fighter. What's gotten into you?"

"Sense. Sense has gotten into me, finally, on the eve of disaster."

She pulled back to stare through the gloom at the scowl creasing his brow. "Nothing—and I mean *nothing*, Spence—must prevent your finishing the church collection in the way you want to, at the pace you choose. It's going to be magnificent, but you'll never be ready for it until I'm off the scene and you can do it your own way. I wish you would have stuck by your convictions from the start and told me to go to the moon when I started interfering. I know you would have, except that you're kind and generous and—" her voice broke "—and you fell in love with me."

"I'm not letting you throw away a career that means the world to you over something I don't give a damn about."

"That's not true. Your work means everything to you."

"*You* mean everything to me. My work is separate, a thing apart."

"It isn't, Spence. You have to stop categorizing your life and your devotion to your art and what you feel for me. They're all a part of the same power and drive that makes a photograph by Spencer Gallant sing and sizzle. You're not doing calendar art. You're creating masterpieces with your whole self. And every photograph with your name on it that hangs in the Ware Gallery has to exemplify that. I convinced myself for a few days that I could let you sell yourself short to save my job, but I can't, Spence."

She closed her eyes on his cool skin. "Though I

love you all the more for wanting to. You could never have given me a more precious gift, but I won't accept. I never should have put you in the position of having to offer."

"I didn't *have* to do anything."

"I know." She whispered against his face. "You're like your sister. Neither one of you knows when it's time to look out for yourself, and that's why I fell in love with you."

He held her tightly. "If you love me you'll let the show go on. It will be all right, Nan. You'll see."

"Please, darling, don't make this any harder than it is. I guess we both knew from the start that we were traveling different roads." She scraped her tongue through her dry mouth to form the words she knew she had to say. "They ran parallel for a brief, lovely while, but now we have to move on."

"Move on to where?" The incredulous look on his face showed he was just beginning to understand that she was calling off more than the show.

"To the stars for you." She drew back her wet face to force a smile through the darkness. "Oh, you don't know how I'm going to glory in your ascent. When the time does come for your show you'll knock Boston on its ear—and then the whole country, the whole world. For you, the sky is the limit."

He moved quietly away from her. "Where will you be?"

"Earthbound, doing what I do best—organizing, setting up shows for talented people." Her throat closed. "And minding my own business better than I did on P.E.I., I hope." She licked the tears off her lips. "Maybe one day I'll have my own gallery and I'll come knocking on your door again to remind you that I knew you when."

He stopped her, his voice wracked with pain. "Is saying goodbye what you really want, Nan?"

Through the haze of her pain she recalled his words about Josey. *People do what they want to do.* If she could make him believe those words now, he would let her go. "Yes, Spence. It's what I want."

But the dam that held back her passion fractured suddenly. She saw the long future without him, and with a starved cry she came into his arms to claim the last crumbs of what sense and love were denying her forever. In the fierce outpouring that followed they clung together, closing out the darkness around them and lighting their hearts with the brilliant, final glow of a dying comet.

15

THE DAY OF JOSEY'S WEDDING dawned bright and clear. During the night the first heavy snow had fallen, and Nan spent the morning packing and going back and forth to the wide sweep of windows that looked out on a beach coated with three inches of confectioner's sugar.

Christmas was only a few days away, and then January would move in with more winter storms, providing the really-deep snow for moonlight toboggan parties and horse-drawn sleigh rides, romantically punctuated by tinkling bells and furry lap robes. In Boston she would be tramping alone through the sidewalk slush, looking for a job.

What she was giving up crowded her thoughts, and everywhere she went Spence's blue-eyed gaze seemed to follow her. Twice she had to stop herself at the door to keep from rushing out to find him.

They had agreed—sensibly, she thought—not to meet again until the wedding.

"We'll never be able to manage any other

way," Nan had begged, and Spence had finally acquiesced. But as the morning dragged on, the prospect of taking up her old life and leaving the new one behind grew increasingly painful.

To keep from falling apart she concentrated pressing out all the imaginary wrinkles in her georgette dress and then pressing them out all over again. She emptied everything out of her refrigerator except the milk for her breakfast, and she still had an hour before it was time to leave for the farm.

But once she was dressed and on the way, skimming past the white fields dotted with crows, her heart lifted a little. This was Josey's wedding day, a fairy-tale day of crystalline sparkles in the meadows and tinkling, ice-clogged streams. She promised herself always to remember the island as it looked now and when she thought of Spence to picture him in the same carefree mood that had captured the day.

Those positive thoughts enabled her to put on a frail smile when she turned off the main road, and the smile was reinforced by the Fox Haven Farm sign Beau had posted at the foot of the lane and by the joy she felt in her heart for Josey and him.

But when she rang the bell and Spence opened the door, tall and solemn in his new suit, her smile died on her lips and it was October again, golden and crisp all around her, and all the days

of loving Spence waited ahead. Except that they
didn't. In a few hours the most precious time of
her life would be over.

Without a word, he pulled her into the hall
and held her close.

Nan clung to the strong arms enfolding her.
Finally she tried to joke. "You have to let me go,
darling. I can't cry and ruin my makeup."

When he drew back his blue eyes were glistening, too. "Parting isn't the answer to anything,
Nan."

"Don't—please." She didn't dare look at him.
"We're upset now, but when we were calmer
you saw my point. I'm not good for you."

She slipped past him into the parlor. White
roses flown in from the mainland decked the
spinet and breathed their perfume to every corner of the room. The bouquet Nan was to carry
lay on a table, an old-fashioned nosegay of lilac-
streamered ribbons and tight little buds of
burgundy roses mixed with baby's breath.

"This is Josey's day," she said when he approached her again. "We can't let what we're
feeling spoil things for her."

She desperately sought another topic. "Tell
me your plans. Tell me where you're moving."

"After you run away," he said steadily, "I'm
moving into your beach house."

A pinching pain in her chest almost made her
cry out. He would lie in her bed and smell the

perfume of her body lingering on the pillows and the bedspread...missing her...wanting her as she wanted him now. It was too cruel, too unfair.

She turned away and fussed with the white satin that covered the makeshift altar in front of the hearth. "Where are Beau and Josey going on their honeymoon?"

"To Toronto. I'm driving them to the airport after the reception."

"I should go upstairs and see if Josey needs me."

"*I* need you," he answered hoarsely, taking her in his arms again. "Don't lock me out, Nan."

She took his kiss. *The last one,* her heartbeat drummed.

Then Cate and Beau came into the room.

Flustered, Nan pulled away. Spence straightened his tie.

"Pardon us for our terrible timing," Cate said lightly.

Beau appeared too numbed by the impending ceremony to notice anything except the clock on the mantel ticking the minutes away.

He cast a wild eye at Spence. "What do you suppose has happened to the minister?"

Spence answered gruffly. "We'll go out on the porch and have a look down the lane."

When the front door closed behind them, Cate turned to Nan. "I'm sorry we barged in."

"It doesn't matter." Nan twisted her handkerchief. "Have you brought the cake? I'd love to see it."

But when they were standing in the kitchen looking down at the pretty white confection decked with dainty lilies-of-the-valley and circled by pink candles Nan quickly ran out of compliments. All she could think of was Spence's white face as he went out with Beau.

Cate seemed to read her mind. "Poor old Spence. He's taking Josey's flight from the nest harder than I thought he would."

Nan swallowed. "I imagine he's feeling very protective."

Then they exchanged the kind of frank look that had characterized the lunch they had shared together and Nan said in a rush of words, "When I leave tomorrow, Cate, I'm not coming back."

"Then it's all over between you and Spence?" Cate waited, letting the sounds of her voice die out in the silence. "I'm sorry. I thought you were so perfectly suited."

Nan held herself rigidly. "In many ways we aren't."

Cate's speculative gaze moved over her. "Are they important ways?"

"They're important to me."

"What does Spence think?"

"You'll have to ask Spence for the answer to that."

"And run the knife through his wounds again?" Cate said softly. She shook her head. "I'd never do that."

Nan brought her chin up and worked to hold back her tears. "I suppose you'd never leave him, either."

"Not if he loved me the way he loves you."

"Love isn't everything."

"Perhaps it isn't." Cate smiled sadly. "But it would be enough for me."

UPSTAIRS IN THE BEDROOM that had been Josey's all her life Nan waited beside her for the first sounds of the wedding march to come from the spinet.

"You're the perfect picture of a bride, Josey."

"I feel bridelike," Josey answered simply. "I only hope I live up to what Beau has dreamed of all these years."

"He'll find you a hundred times more lovely than he ever imagined."

Nan admired Josey's calm, especially since her own heart was thumping like a wild bird in a cage. On her way up she had passed Spence on the stairs. The hall below was crowded with arriving guests and they could only pause to look at each other, but the moment lasted long enough for her to feel the full brunt of Spence's piercing gaze. Then he moved on, leaving her unnerved and trembling and more acutely aware than ever that the grains in their hourglass had all but run out.

Gazing now at Josey, she longed with every fiber of her being to be as radiant and confident and joyous as Josey was. As far as it was possible for anyone to know what the future held, Josey and Beau knew. They had common goals; they were settled and secure. She was only a few years younger than Josey, but nothing in her life had any direction except her work, and now even that seemed without foundation.

Josey smiled. "I won't tell you again because I know you're tired of hearing it, but I'll never forget, Nan, that you made this wedding possible—and I won't stop hoping, either, that one of these days you'll be my sister-in-law."

"Oh, Josey," Nan choked, "not now, please. You don't want a teary maid-of-honor."

"You're a beautiful maid-of-honor, and if Spence can't see that and do something about it before it's too late—"

Nan interrupted. "Listen—isn't that the music?" They both turned toward the strains of Lohengrin floating up the stairs.

Josey took a last quick look in the mirror and kissed Nan on the cheek. "This is it!" she said with shining eyes. "I'll wait until you reach the landing and then I'll follow."

THE SWEET, SIMPLE CEREMONY in the parlor enthralled Nan in a way she hadn't expected.

The descent down the stairs had presented her

with the customary heart flutters and damp palms all wedding attendants experienced, and she wasn't surprised that Spence at the foot, waiting for her, quickened again her yearning. But from the moment the minister began to speak, reminding Beau and Josey of the seriousness of their vows, her whole focus was on the bride and groom.

Her mind began to go back over the long, twisted road the two of them had traveled to reach the point of matrimony . . . Josey's looking out for her mother first . . . Beau's unfortunate marriage. Then there were the years Josey had dedicated herself to Spence.

Mechanically Nan took the bouquet Josey held out to her. Upstairs she had envied Josey because her life seemed settled and secure. But the minister's words reminded her that no one's life was ever that way. No one knew from one moment to the next what the future held.

Trembling, she watched Beau tenderly slipping a gold ring onto Josey's finger. In spite of the uncertainties that lay ahead, these two were plighting their troth, stepping out into the unknown together because, beyond all their difficulties, love shone brighter than anything else.

The miracle of the wedding ceremony, Nan saw suddenly, was not that it promised unending happiness, but that it signified unending trust, a circle of faith like the ring Josey wore . . . trust in each other no matter what challenges might threaten. Together they could conquer them.

Nan's eyes went to Spence, standing tall and solemn at Beau's side. For a moment their glances locked, and Nan had the dizzy sensation he was sharing her thoughts. If only she and Spence could have discovered the same kind of magic that bound Josey and Beau together...if only they could turn the calendar back to October and begin again....

The ceremony ended. The guests in the parlor came out of their seats and rushed forward with exclamations and kisses of congratulations for Mr. and Mrs. Beauregard Bonnell.

Nan waited a minute, hoping Spence would turn to her, but he blended with the crowd. In another minute she saw him go over to Cate and escort her toward the dining room.

When everyone had gathered around the table, Spence raised a toast to the bride and groom. Champagne glasses clinked. Then the birthday candles were lit, and Josey made her wish and blew them all out. Nan was busy after that, helping to see that the guests were served and the wineglasses refilled. Whenever she had a chance she glanced around for Spence, but his eyes were never searching for her.

Sooner than she expected, Josey was coming down the stairs in her blue wool traveling suit.

Someone called out, "You've forgotten to throw your bouquet."

But Josey ducked out as if she hadn't heard. Nan wondered if she was the only person left in the crowded room who knew why, until her gaze met Cate's, quiet and steady above a wistful smile.

Except for the two of them, all the female guests were married. By omitting the customary gesture of tossing her bouquet, Josey had mercifully spared them a contest that both of them had already lost.

By the time Spence had returned from seeing the wedding couple off on their plane, everyone had left except Nan and Cate, who were helping the caterers put the finishing touches to the cleanup. When Cate spotted Spence's car headed up the lane, she said goodbye to Nan and disappeared discreetly through the back door as Spence came in the front.

Trapped in the hallway, Nan stood awkwardly before him, her fingers sticky with a dollop of white icing she had scooped up from the floor.

"Are the bride and groom on their way?"

Spence nodded and hung his coat over the newel. "What are you doing?"

Grateful for a reason to avert her gaze, she glanced at her sticky fingers. "Until I ran into this I was straightening up a little."

"Has everyone else gone?"

"Everyone but the caterers—and they're packing up." She moved toward the dining room, doing her best to hide the sense of desolation that cloaked her. "I'm leaving, too, as soon as I wash my hands."

Spence followed her. "It seems to me this is where we came in."

"What?" A note in his voice that was reminiscent of happier days turned her around. "What do you mean?"

"Icing." He lowered his tone to a husky murmur. "Remember? With a teaspoon of almond extract and a drop of peppermint."

She had been remembering all day. Swallowing, she took a shivering breath. "We've come full circle, haven't we?" She waited for the dull pounding of her heart to subside. "Will you come over in the morning to say goodbye before I leave for the ferry?"

He rubbed a smudge from the shiny surface of a table at his side. "I'm not much for goodbyes."

The emptiness inside her widened. From across the gulf that separated them she said in a barely audible voice, "Can we just walk away from each other without saying anything?"

He looked directly at her. "Isn't that the way you wanted it?" The blue of his eyes absorbed her, pulling her into their depths. "The last time the subject came up you had all the details of your life in neat compartments tied with red ribbon."

Nan stayed silent, unable to meet his gaze for fear her tears would spill over.

After a minute Spence said, "I have to pay the caterer. Wait for me in the parlor."

When Spence found Nan again she had washed the sticky icing off her hands and was picking out a few lonely notes on the spinet.

He waited until she was finished, and when she turned around, her eyes bright with unshed tears, he said, "Come and sit down."

He motioned her toward the sofa, and she recalled with a twisting pain that he was pointing out the same spot where she had sat down the first day she arrived on the island.

He had worn an apron that October day. She hadn't known what to make of him except that even in that dubious moment he had excited her. She had been drawn as she was drawn now to his eminently kissable mouth and his granite chin and his heavy brow. Something in her had recognized destiny even while the smell of chocolate cake floated through the house and half her thoughts were still on David Pryor.

Her trembling knees gave way and she sank gratefully onto the needlepoint cushion. Spence, too, seemed to remember that brilliant fall day and took his place in the chair across from her.

"'Full circle,'" he said, repeating her earlier statement. "Has it occurred to you that circles are never ending?"

Like wedding rings. Nan's heartbeat quickened. Then abruptly he stood up again.

"There's a bottle of champagne left in the kitchen. Let's take it up to the loft."

Champagne . . . when what she wanted was to be held in his arms . . . to be told again how much he loved her. She got out of her chair. "I'd like to see the loft once more."

But following him up the stairs, she wished she had refused his invitation. The studio loft was where their love had begun. The irony of having it end there, too, was almost too much to bear.

As they climbed toward the top of the house its smells rose around them, familiar and dear. Spice from Josey's potpourri, the scents of old linen and old books, of ancient wallpaper and lemony floor wax. Nan recalled the dark stairwell at her aunt's farm in Wisconsin and felt a forlorn ten again, trailing after Spence through a house that was no longer his, on an island that would never be hers.

Just before they reached the loft he paused and turned around to give her a look she couldn't decipher. "You'll be surprised at what you find inside."

"Why?" For an instant curiosity displaced her depression. She crowded close as he opened the door. Then she saw that the objects she loved and had become accustomed to were gone. The Toltec statue, the lobster pots—even the cunning little carved birds in their make-believe marsh. Gone. All gone.

The room was bare, except that splashed across the walls were dozens of photographs—large ones, small ones—in every dimension, in every pose. All photographs of her.

She halted, stunned.

The effect was overwhelming. But not overwhelming in the way it would have been in the hands of a lesser craftsman than Spence. Instead of the gross monotony that should have been the natural result of the same face repeated again and again, the features the photographs shared served as compelling links, casting a spell over her.

The repetition of nose and eyes and chin and cheek was what held the whole display together, and running through in bright, passionate threads that lit up the airy space containing them were the vibrancy of laughter, the piquancy of curiosity, gaiety, anger, concentration, joyous abandon.... There weren't names enough for all the emotions and mixtures of emotions the prints depicted.

Gazing around in a rapturous silence, Nan realized there was no more sameness to the prints than the words of a language occurring again and again in sentences that never turned out the same. A thrill stirred deep inside her and swelled, until a single word that made up a book of sentences came spilling over her lips.

"Woman—" She turned around with fascinated wonder to stare at Spence. "I hope that's what you're going to call it—'Woman.'"

"'It'?" From the other side of the room where he had been watching her, Spence inquired softly, "And what is 'it,' Nan?"

Goose bumps sped up her spine and she whirled, watching the prints race by. "It's a show—a magnificent, marvelous show of shows!" Her gaze turned starry. "It's the boldest, the most daring, most innovative arrangement of work I've ever seen—"

And then she gave up trying to express what the photographs were already saying so well and turned back to inspecting every face, all so alike and so different, so unique and so universal.

"Oh, Spence—" She stopped again at his side.

Looking down at her, he said quietly, "Is it good enough for the Ware Gallery?"

"You know it is," she answered reverently. "It's good enough for the Louvre."

He set down the champagne bottle. "Then I guess our problem is solved."

Her heart took a leap as she dared to consider what his words might imply.

Spence went on. "You don't have to rush back to Boston in sackcloth and ashes to confess failure to Remington Ware. We have our show."

Her gaze jumped back to the prints hanging on the wall. "Me, instead of the churches?"

Reaching out swiftly, he pulled her into his arms. "The churches aren't ready to take their

bow in public. You are. And you don't ever have
to worry again that you're bad for me. If seventy-
five prints don't prove that you're my inspiration, I don't know what will."

Joy almost choked her. "I can't believe this.
Downstairs—"

"Downstairs there was a wedding this afternoon. I looked at you and knew I could never let
you go, not for a month, not for five minutes."

Tears filled her eyes. "Oh, my darling—"

"Didn't you know? Didn't you feel the electricity between us?"

"For a moment during the ceremony I did."
She clung to him. "Then you ignored me completely."

"I had no choice. If I had come anywhere near
you I would have made a public declaration right
there in the parlor, and what do you imagine
Josey's Bible circle would have thought?"

An ecstatic burst of laughter exploded from
her throat. "I think they would have loved it."
She brought his head down and covered his
mouth with kisses. "*I* would have loved it. I'm
loving it now. Tell me more."

"Later, my love." He swung her up in his arms.
"The Bible circle has gone home. The house is
ours."

THEY HAD NEVER made love in Spence's bed before. It was narrow and four postered and high
off the floor.

"What if we fall out of here?" Nan questioned giddily.

Spence put his mouth to the soft, sweet curve of her body. "I don't expect to notice."

IT WAS MORNING before they talked seriously again, trailing hand in hand through the packed snow down to the frozen duck pond.

Nan leaned against Spence's shoulder. "How long has it been since I told you I love you?"

"Far too long. Five minutes at least." He nuzzled her cheek.

"How careless of me." She kissed his freshly shaved cheek and said, "Tonight I'll write *I love you* a hundred times and put the paper beneath your pillow."

"While you're doing that," he answered thickly, "I'll take your picture in that funny little high-topped nightgown you were wearing when I photographed you in bed."

The photograph Spence had taken of her while she slept in her cottage was the focal point of the new show. Spence's careful composition shadowed most of her body, but enough seductive curves were revealed to create a sensuous study of "Woman" in a most vulnerable state. Nan was thrilled to be the subject of so lovely a portrait, but she wasn't used to the idea of appearing in public not quite dressed.

"You may have too many pictures of me already," she said. "Rem will have a stroke as it is when he finds out it won't be churches filling up his gallery on the twenty-first."

"He knows." Spence dug his hands into the pockets of his jacket. "I telephoned him yesterday at the airport to tell him I'd switched subjects."

Nan shook her head in disbelief. "How many more surprises do you have concealed up your fleece-lined sleeve?"

Frowning, he consulted the blue sky. "Only one more, I think." He darted a look at her. "I don't believe I've mentioned that we're getting married."

Nan stopped still in the pathway. " 'Married.' " Her lips parted. "Who?"

"You and I, Nan." He laughed at her stunned look. "We *have* to, darling." Leaning over, he kissed the tip of her nose. "What will I do with this ring if we don't?"

From his pocket he pulled a gleaming circle of gold and held it out to her. "My father gave this to my mother forty-two years ago on Christmas Day."

"Your parents' wedding ring." Nan stared down at it. "How beautiful—and how precious!"

"There's room inside for our inscription beside theirs—unless we have to size it smaller." He closed the ring into her palm, murmuring huskily, "My bride's fingers are so tiny."

" 'Married.' " Tears of happiness rolled down

Nan's cheeks. "Spence, I never thought...
you've never said...."

His lips came down to cover hers. "I'm a man
of few words. Haven't you noticed?"

In his arms she noticed everything—the cold,
clean smell of him and his wide, protecting
shoulders and the way he held her, as if he never
meant to let her go. Her fingers tangled in his
springy hair; her body swayed with his.

"'Married,'" she said again when finally he
did let her go. "In the parlor, Spence?" Her
words tumbled out as her excitement grew.
"With burgundy roses? And white gladioli, and
ivy on the mantel?"

"With whatever you want." He feasted on her
sparkling eyes and rosy cheeks. "As long as
there's a minister who knows how to tie a knot
that can never be untied."

"Oh, Spence—I love you!"

"And I love you, Nan." He gazed down at
her, rapt with adoration. "You taught me it's
not enough to float along like flotsam in the sea.
Life's too short for drifting. I have to get on with
my work, and now I can because I'll have you at
my side." Suddenly the laughter she loved
glinted in his eyes. "God knows I waited long
enough for you to come along and prod me with
your barbed stick."

"And my barbed tongue," she teased ruefully.
"I'll bet you're still smarting."

"At least I've mended the worst of my ways." He grew serious again. "But I can't promise revolutionary changes in what I've been all my life." He traced her cheekbone with the back of his thumb. "I have an idea I'll always need to fall into trances in churchyards and stare at the sky. I'll always want to do things on the spur of the moment. My slipshod ways may drive you out of your orderly mind. But I'll be loving you, Nan, with all my heart for the rest of my days."

"Oh, my darling—" She raised shining eyes to his. "That's all I'll ever need." Then suddenly her shyness peeked out and deepened the rosy hue of her cheeks. "Except for one more thing, something silly and old-fashioned, but very important."

Spence groaned. "If you're going to ask me to sleep in a nightcap, I won't do it."

She punched him playfully. "That's not it, you ridiculous oaf." She hesitated and then blurted it out in one long breath. "Could you get down on your knees and make a proper proposal?"

Spence stared. "Here, do you mean? In the snow?" She nodded, and he spluttered, "That's not old-fashioned—that's medieval!"

But he knelt, anyway, and took her hands in his. "Will you do me the honor of marrying me, Nan Blake?"

A row of quacking ducks came out of the willows and waddled past, but Nan was oblivious to everything except the sweet huskiness of his voice falling gently on her ears.

"Yes, my precious one, I will." She raised her hands to lift him up. "Yes, a thousand times! Yes, with love!"

TAKE THESE 4 FREE
Harlequin Romances

Delight in **Mary Wibberley**'s warm romance, MAN OF POWER, the story of a girl whose life changes from drudgery to glamour overnight....Let THE WINDS OF WINTER by **Sandra Field** take you on a journey of love to Canada's beautiful Maritimes....Thrill to a cruise in the tropics—and a devastating love affair in the aftermath of a shipwreck—in **Rebecca Stratton**'s THE LEO MAN.... Travel to the wilds of Kenya in a quest for love with the determined heroine in **Karen van der Zee**'s LOVE BEYOND REASON.

Harlequin Romances ... 6 exciting novels published each month! Each month you will get to know interesting, appealing, true-to-life people .... You'll be swept to distant lands you've dreamed of visiting .... Intrigue, adventure, romance, and the destiny of many lives will thrill you through each Harlequin Romance novel.

Get all the latest books before they're sold out!

As a Harlequin subscriber you actually receive your personal copies of the latest Romances immediately after they come off the press, so you're sure of getting all 6 each month.

Cancel your subscription whenever you wish!

You don't have to buy any minimum number of books. Whenever you decide to stop your subscription just let us know and we'll cancel all further shipments.